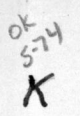

BLOODWATER

Buena Costa County Mysteries by the Same Author

ANOTHER WAY TO DIE
A TOUCH OF DARKNESS

BLOODWATER

John Crowe

A BUENA COSTA COUNTY MYSTERY

DODD, MEAD & COMPANY · NEW YORK

Copyright © 1974 by John Crowe
All rights reserved
No part of this book may be reproduced in any form
without permission in writing from the publisher

ISBN: 0-396-06947-9
Library of Congress Catalog Card Number: 74-101
Printed in the United States of America
by Vail-Ballou Press, Inc., Binghamton, N.Y.

To Charley

1

Celia Pearson screamed.

The scream blew away across the sunny Monteverde airport on a blast of jet engines. A tall, bone-thin woman in her forties, Celia Pearson swayed in the jet stream of the departing northbound 727. Her husband, who had been watching her, caught her before she could fall.

"Celia!"

James Pearson motioned to his son. Alan Pearson jumped to support his mother. The Japanese girl stood back. A tiny girl, no more than nineteen, she had a round face, full hips and heavy black eyes. She watched the Pearsons like someone observing strange animals in some zoo.

"Take me home," Celia Pearson said.

"Alan," James Pearson said, "you and your friend go and get your bags. We'll be in the car."

A tall man in a dark gray business suit, Pearson's calm blue eyes had authority. The roar of the departing jet had covered Celia Pearson's scream from most of the passengers still leaving the southbound 727 in the January sun. Only two men and a woman directly behind Alan Pearson noticed. The woman, a narrow-faced blonde in a black-and-white designer coat, turned to look. One of the men hurried to the Pearsons.

"Jim?" the man said. "Something wrong?"

"Just too much noise and excitement, Sam."

Short and muscular in a gaudy yellow blazer, the newcomer looked at Alan Pearson. "Saw Alan and the girl on the plane. A little surprise, kid?"

"Not exactly, Mr. Garnet," the boy said. His face was thin and intelligent behind horn-rimmed glasses.

Celia Pearson, limp against her husband, stared at her son and Sam Garnet. A fixed stare. She closed her eyes.

"I wanted you to meet Jitsuko first, Dad," Alan said.

"It's all right," James Pearson said. "Now let's go—"

Celia Pearson opened her eyes, glared around the open space of the airport in the windy January sunlight. She saw the Japanese girl. She smiled at her.

"How long have you been in our country, my dear?" Celia Pearson said, almost eagerly. She looked down at her husband's arms that held her. "My goodness, let go of me, Jim. Holding me in public! That's not like you at all."

"Mother?" Alan said. "You're all right?"

"All right?" She looked surprised, bright-eyed. "Of course I'm all right. Now stop it, both of you! What will your friend think?" She saw Sam Garnet. "Sam, where did you appear from?"

"On the same plane with Alan, Celia," Sam Garnet said.

Celia Pearson turned to the girl. "Have you been in the country long, my dear?"

"A few months only," the Japanese girl said, her English with a trace of accent. "I hope I have not disturbed you."

"There!" Celia glared at the men. "Of course you haven't disturbed us. We're delighted." She held her hand out. "I'm Celia Pearson."

The girl took the offered hand.

"I am Jitsuko Ikeda," she said.

She smiled more at the men than at Celia Pearson.

*

George Thesiger drove irritably. On a business trip with Sam Garnet, he and his wife had been with Garnet when Celia Pearson screamed. Now they drove behind Garnet and the Pearsons into Monteverde. Anne Thesiger held her designer coat closed.

"Christ," she said, "a gook girl. Celia got a shock."

"Shut up," George Thesiger said.

"Swell!" The narrow-faced blonde woman watched the two cars ahead on the freeway. "So the Japs get the whole company someday. *My* company!"

"Jesus," Thesiger said, "they're kids! Kids don't marry everyone they bring home these days; they shack up."

"Alan? The good boy?"

"Okay, Anne, enjoy yourself."

They rode in silence. A heavy-set man of medium height, well-dressed and in his late forties, with wavy gray hair and the public face of a real-estate man. The woman small and big-breasted under her narrow face, her posture showing the breasts.

"Our company, too," Anne said. "It should be. You had to let Sam Garnet take your place."

"And welcome to it," Thesiger said. "You knew I didn't want regular hours, company organization, or Hook Instrument."

"I'm older now. Twenty years older. And you work for Sam Garnet."

"With Sam Garnet," Thesiger said. "I work *with* Sam,

partners. Okay? My own boss."

"Junior partner. You run a saloon."

"A restaurant, damn it. One in ten properties because someone has to manage an inn, and Sam's got his regular work at Hook!" Thesiger turned off the freeway behind the other two cars. "Look, stop the record, okay? It's the game day, I want a shower and a nice drink before I go."

Anne Thesiger shrank into her coat, watched the big houses of the Monteverde suburbs.

*

Monteverde is the second largest city of Buena Costa County. In the north-center of the county, it sits on the Monteverde Plateau a thousand feet above sea level ringed by mountains. North, east and south the Coast Range fills eighty percent of the county. West, the Santa Rosa spur-range blocks the sea breezes, except for a gently sloping corridor to the coast and the capital city of San Vicente in the south.

In 1902, at the end of the Boer War in South Africa, Andreas Hoek packed up his rifles, wife and brood and took ship at Delagoa Bay. A true Afrikaner, he spoke to a private God, and considered the universe to exist for his immediate family only. All other people were alien and enemy, to be used as the cattle he bred or the lions he shot.

A Boer even more recalcitrant than most, he had one goal—to find cattle land far from the hated British Crown. Since he had sailed to the east, this brought him to California. From Los Angeles he drove a wagon north into rural Buena Costa County, crossed Mesa Grande Pass, and looked down on the Monteverde Plateau. He saw a miracle.

Flat, brown and dusty—cut by dry creek beds and dotted with low hills—the plateau shimmered in heat under a high sky. A single railroad line, and a shallow river, wandered in and out of the town of Monteverde itself, that was like a hundred *dorps* north of the Orange River. Small and bare, the town lay dwarfed by sky and distance as if dropped on the plain for no apparent reason, in imminent danger of blowing away without trace.

To Andreas Hoek it was his lost high *veld*, and he loved it.

He bought his farm north of town on the only creek that always had water, and named it Brandwater after his old *veld* basin. He named the creek The Vaal, and raised prize cattle, six sons, and five daughters. He was escaping both the British and the twentieth century, but he was too late.

The highways came. Cities had to be fed, business grew, industry boomed, and the land was too valuable for cattle. Too many people moved in, Monteverde became the center of northern Buena Costa County. A yellow brick city of busy main streets and crowded tracts, of bowling alley and supermarket. Without shade or beauty, it beats to the pulse of commerce and real estate, and Andreas Hoek is gone. Trekked on long ago into Nevada with his cattle, his rifles, and his brood.

But he left his mark. His old farm, now the richest suburb of Monteverde, is still called Brandwater. The creek is still Vaal Creek, and old Andreas's last son still lives on its banks. As individual as Andreas himself, Cornelius Hoek changed his name to Hook, left farming to found Hook Instrument Company, and never heard from a Hoek again, or they from him.

All the older houses in Brandwater are big under dusty eucalyptus trees. Cornelius Hook's big house stands on a hill above Vaal Creek. This January afternoon seven men gathered in the glass-walled study for old Hook's bi-monthly poker game. George Thesiger, Sam Garnet (Hook Instrument's vice-president of Personnel and Plant Security), Captain Vause of the Monteverde Police Department, County Prosecutor Charles Tucker, and Dr. Lowell Fynn were at the green table playing.

James Pearson, president of Hook Instrument, was at the far end of the sunny room with Cornelius Hook, his board chairman and father-in-law. The old man lit a cigar.

"Is Celia all right now?" Hook asked.

"Fynn gave her a sedative; she's resting."

"Not the start of a spell? It's been a long time, Jim."

Pearson sighed. "I'd thought it was all over for good."

"Was it that girl? What's her name? Ikeda?"

"Jitsuko Ikeda. I suppose it was that."

"Alan's new girl, eh?" Cornelius Hook studied the ash on his cigar. "Anything else to tell me, Jim?"

"No. I'll just watch her."

"Fine," Hook said. "You've been a good husband, Jim, and a good executive. Remember that. Now let's play some poker."

They played all afternoon. Each man made his own drinks out in Hook's living room. Twice, James Pearson and Sam Garnet made drinks together. Garnet joined both Hook and George Thesiger once. When the game ended at four-thirty, a detective picked up Captain Vause. Sam Garnet asked for a lift.

"Hook drove me over," Garnet explained. "We'll stop for a drink at my place. Some thirty-year-old Scotch I've got."

*

"Good stuff," Captain Vause said.

A dapper man in glasses, Vause sat at the bar in Garnet's

game room. Detective-Sergeant Harry Wood carried his drink as he looked around the house.

"Like it, Wood?" Sam Garnet asked.

Torn out and rebuilt, the walls were painted in loud colors like a Mondrian abstract. Thick drapes covered the windows, carpet muffled the floors. There was a single large bedroom downstairs, and no living room. What had been the living room was an indoor swimming pool surrounded by chairs, couches and green plants like a tropical oasis. The game room had two pool tables and a poker table. A bachelor's house.

"A long way from being a cop, Mr. Garnet," Wood said.

Ten years younger than Vause or Garnet, the Sergeant was a slow-spoken man, his black hair already balding. Slightly stooped, he seemed shorter than his six feet, and older than thirty-eight.

"Sometimes I wish I was back on the force," Garnet said.

"No you don't," Wood said.

Garnet smiled. "Maybe not." He drank. "I'd be captain by now, though. Regular hours, paper work. No coming home from one trip and taking right off on another."

"You had two years on me," Vause said. "Captain at least."

Garnet shrugged. "You make a choice, right? Hook needed a security chief, triple pay. I took it."

"You made the right choice," Wood said, finished his whisky.

"I guess I did," Sam Garnet said, drained his glass. "Well, I'm off to L.A. again. Thanks for the lift."

*

The River Inn is a large roadhouse a mile west of Monteverde where the freeway to the coast curves along the

Santa Rosa River. George Thesiger managed the Inn as a partner in River Enterprises, Inc. At five-thirty, Thesiger was in his office with a big, long-haired young man. Sam Garnet walked in carrying a suitcase. George Thesiger scowled at the suitcase.

"Another damned trip? So soon?"

"Vice-presidents never sleep. Anne bugging you again?"

"It's the Inn, too low-class," Thesiger said. "Maybe we can get a manager. How about Tugela there?"

Garnet looked at the younger man. "You want to run a restaurant, Vinnie?"

Vinnie Tugela lounged in a chair tilted against the wall, his long legs stretched out in stained corduroys. He had a lazy, youthful face with a thick mustache, and an athletic body. His long hair, mustache and rough clothes made him look younger than he was. Thirty, his eyes deep in wind wrinkles.

"I like your boat, Mr. Garnet. Maybe the casino."

"Don't get greedy, Vinnie." Garnet grinned, turned back to Thesiger. "We'll talk about it, George. Right now I want Tugela to run me to the airport. Be back in a few days."

*

At midnight there was still a light in the Pearson house in Brandwater, and in the guest cottage. Jitsuko Ikeda lay on the bed in the guest cottage. Naked under a red kimono, she was a tiny girl but full-bodied, curved. Alan Pearson bent to kiss her. She stroked his hair.

"Your family is nice, Alan," the girl said. "Rich, yes? A fine house. But something is wrong, I think."

"It's Mother. She isn't very strong, has breakdowns. When I was real young, she used to go down to a sanitarium all the time. She was there for months after I was born."

"I'm sorry," Jitsuko said. "Your father worries for her?"

"I guess so, but he's always busy. The family company, Hook Instrument. My grandfather owns it, mostly, but Dad and Sam Garnet run it. Old army buddies, my father and Garnet."

"All work," Jitsuko said. "Your father's generation."

"Let's talk about us, Suko. I guess I'm in love with you."

"So soon?" She smiled up at him. "Tomorrow we can talk about it. I am tired now."

It was almost one A.M. when Alan left. Jitsuko turned out the lights in the cottage. She didn't go to bed. She went to a window and watched Alan Pearson get into his white Porsche and drive off. The girl smiled—Alan didn't want to sleep after leaving her. Then she saw the car.

An old, dark-colored Buick parked in the shadows of the street. Jitsuko watched the Buick until nearly two-thirty when Alan returned, and the last light went out in the big house. The Buick didn't move. Until three A.M. Then it drove away.

Jitsuko Ikeda dressed, went out into the cold night, and walked away down the dark Brandwater street.

2

It had started to rain when the squad car called in the murder at the El Prado Motel. Detective-Sergeant Harry Wood put on his slicker and drove to the run-down motel near the railroad tracks and the freeway. Two squad cars were parked at a rear unit in the rain. A patrolman waited with the manager under the office awning out of the rain.

The manager was a fat man in a raincoat over pants and undershirt. "Maybe two A.M. I thought I heard something. Like shots. I was asleep, groggy, and who knows from shots here?"

The manager waved at the freeway traffic and the railroad.

"A transient, Sarge," the patrolman said. "Paul Tracy. His driver's license shows a San Diego address, but his car's an L.A. rental. Car's clean, no ident except the license."

"When did he come in?" Wood said.

"About one A.M., woke me up," the manager said. "Place is almost empty. I didn't hear nothin' more, went back to sleep."

"Who found him?"

"Maid. Forgot to tell her the unit was booked."

"Did he do anything? Have visitors? Go out?"

"Couple o' cars drove in. I was in bed. He made a call out. Local. I gave him a line, he dialed it himself."

Wood and the patrolman went back to the rear unit. The second patrolman met them at the door. He looked puzzled. An older patrolman, Jennings, on the force ten years.

"Shot twice, Harry. Gun's in the room. Funny, but I swear I've seen the guy somewhere."

Wood went into the unit. There was no suitcase, and the bed hadn't been slept in. An untouched room. If the man hadn't died here, he might have passed through without a trace. Instead, he lay on his back beside a cheap, bare desk. There was a lot of blood.

"You've seen him," Wood said to Patrolman Jennings. "Go call Captain Vause. Get him down here. Now."

Wood looked down at the dead face of Sam Garnet.

*

Captain Vause watched the Assistant Coroner work over Garnet. Vause licked his lips as if tasting the old Scotch he had drunk in the dead man's house only yesterday afternoon.

"The driver's license has to be a phony," Harry Wood said. "He's wearing a chain-store suit. Nothing in his pockets except five hundred in cash. The gun's his, we've got it on file. I guess he never went to L.A. Or he came back."

"What the hell was he doing here?" Captain Vause said, looked around the bare room. "A place like this?"

"The room's clean, not even a cigarette butt, except for this." Wood held up a small rectangle of black plastic marked with the numbers 100. "We know there's a floating casino out in the county, Captain."

"A gambling killing? Why? Sam was rich."

11

"More like a business murder," Wood said, put the gambling plaque in his pocket. "River Enterprises runs that casino, you know that. Garnet's side operation. I don't think he had that plaque with him, I think someone else dropped it here."

"Maybe," Vause said. The Captain looked around the shabby room again. "A woman, Harry? Meeting her here? It's out of the way, would explain the phony business trip."

"Garnet liked women," Wood said.

The Assistant Coroner wiped his hands on a towel, stood up.

"Two shots, both in front. A thirty-eight looks right."

Diaz, the lab technician, held up the gun. "Smith and Wesson Chiefs Special. It was on the floor. Fired twice."

Wood said, "What time, Doc?"

"About two A.M., give or take. I'll report on the autopsy. No other marks I can see now. Can I take him?"

"Take him," Captain Vause said.

Wood said, "Any signs of entry?"

"All locked up, no marks," Diaz said. "Garnet must have let him in. Someone he knew, I guess."

"Don't guess, Diaz!" Captain Vause snapped.

Diaz shrugged. Harry Wood studied his hands.

"It doesn't have to be anyone he knew," Vause said. "How about a key? An area like this, there's a crook for every motel room. Talk to that manager!"

"I'll talk to him," Wood said.

"Or not the manager. Hell, he was asleep, anyone could lift the key from the office. A setup, maybe, right? Some tramp and her boy friend. Garnet chased any skirt, always did. Set him up here, rob him."

"Sure," Diaz said. "And leave five hundred in his pants."

"Garnet had the room key," Wood said. "The only duplicate is on the manager's chain."

Captain Vause turned to watch the Coroner's men put the body onto a stretcher, cover it, carry it out. There was nothing under the body. Diaz began to work on fingerprints.

"Prints all over," he said. "Except on the gun."

"Take them all," Wood said.

Captain Vause said, "I'll call Tucker and the Sheriff."

"It's a city case," Wood said.

"They should know about it."

"Sure. Hook Instrument throws a lot of weight."

Vause walked out of the unit. Harry Wood listened to the Captain's car screech away through the rain. He felt a certain sympathy for the Captain, a touchy murder. Sam Garnet had been a vice-president, a rich businessman. He'd also been a cop once, and had still known where to get a fake driver's license.

Wood knelt down and studied the floor and worn rug. Blood, almost dry now, and after a time he noticed the trace of machine oil where the pistol had been found. As if Sam Garnet had just oiled his gun. Wood went over the whole room once more. This time he spotted the thin patch of oil on the bare desk. He looked at the oil on the desk for some time.

*

The rain was a steady torrent when Harry Wood tried the front door of Sam Garnet's house in Brandwater. The door was unlocked. Wood pushed it open warily, stepped inside. In the gray light, the gaudy interior looked like a stage-set, and the pool with its lush plants seemed fetid, a swamp. Murder changes the mood.

A door banged somewhere near the game room, a steady banging as if blown on the rain wind. Wood traced it to Sam Garnet's private office off the game room. One panel of the French doors into the garden was open and banging, and the office had been ransacked. Every drawer and filing cabinet searched.

A frantic search, papers and drawers littered everywhere. The French doors had been broken open. Wood took a half hour to probe through the litter. He found only real-estate papers, contracts, stock reports, bank statements, the debris of Sam Garnet's business outside Hook Instrument. If anything was missing, it didn't show, and anything left wouldn't be important.

Wood found the small, blue stone near the desk. About the size of his fingernail, flat on one side. A gemstone from a man's ring. Wood put it into his pocket with the gambling plaque. He couldn't remember Sam Garnet ever wearing a ring.

The thud came from inside the house.

Wood drew his gun.

He heard nothing more.

He stepped lightly through the game room into the pool area. It was still deserted. The dining room was empty, and the kitchen. The bedroom door was closed. Wood pushed it open quickly, slipped inside and to the right. The drapes were drawn, the room gloomy in dim light. There were three large mirrors, thick red carpet, a man's bureau, and an enormous bed.

A woman lay on the bed.

She didn't move. Wood saw the handbag where it had fallen to the floor, and watched her. She lay silent, her eyes hidden in the gloomy light. Her short blue skirt was bunched at her hips, showing long, smooth legs in panty hose. The skirt curved over her hips, and her belly was flat. She opened her eyes.

In the dimness they were dark eyes, staring up. Not afraid, more as if asking a question. She wasn't young, in her thirties somewhere, with dark copper hair and regular features. Her nose a shade too large, a little crooked. Neither tall nor short. A pretty woman, but "pretty" wasn't the word that came to Harry Wood's mind—no word, a feeling, something special.

"He's dead," she said. "Shot."

She moved on the bed as if her bones ached, sat up against the headboard. Wood recognized her now: Alice Garnet, the sister. The rain outside seemed to grow louder. Sometimes you see someone a way you've never seen them before.

"Last night," Wood said. "I'm Detective-Sergeant Wood."

She looked for her handbag. Wood picked it up, gave it to her. She took out a cigarette, lit it, smoked.

"Vause called me," she said. "I knew it had to be a mistake, so I came here. Sam wasn't here. Then I remembered he was in Los Angeles. A business trip."

"He told you he was going?"

"Yes. He stopped by with Vinnie Tugela on his way out."

"He came back."

She closed her eyes again in the dim bedroom.

"You want a drink, Miss Garnet?" Wood said. "Some coffee?"

She nodded. "Coffee, yes. A lot of coffee."

"Can you get up all right?"

She got up, smoothed her mini-dress. It fitted her well. Wood took her arm, but she shook his hand off, walked ahead out of the bedroom and the house. She had a long, mannish stride.

3

In her upstairs bedroom, Celia Pearson stood at a window and watched her son and the Japanese girl run through the rain to his car. Her thin hand was at her throat, squeezing the loose skin in folds.

Over five-feet-nine, she was wasted thin. The bones of her shoulders jutted against the cloth of a thin green robe. Her face had a hawk nose and hollow cheeks, and her eyes were circled by shadow. She looked fifty and tired, only her thick, well-brushed dark hair belonging to a woman of forty-two.

Her window was closed against the rain, but she opened her mouth to call down to her son and the Japanese girl as they got into Alan's white Porsche. She made only a small sound, and shrank back far from the window. She was still staring at the closed window as if it were an enemy when her room door opened behind her.

"Celia?" James Pearson said. "How do you feel? Better this morning?"

"He doesn't have his raincoat," Celia Pearson said. "He'll be sick. He doesn't have a hat."

"Alan? He only ran to his car. That can't hurt him."

Below, the Porsche drove away down the hill.

"A Japanese girl," Celia Pearson said.

"She seems nice enough," James Pearson said.

"Young and pretty," Celia said. "I watched her."

"Alan's nineteen, dear. It's about time he got serious."

"He's like me, not strong." Celia Pearson sat on her bed. "He'll get sick, I know it. Call him back, James."

"He's all right, Celia. He always has been."

She nodded vaguely. "How old is she? The girl?"

"Nineteen, I think," Pearson said, watched his wife.

Celia went on nodding, like some plastic toy. Her hands were in her lap, folded together. James Pearson hesitated.

"Celia," he said, "Sam Garnet was murdered last night."

"Sam Garnet?" Her shadowed eyes frowned. "Murder?"

"Shot in some cheap motel near the railroad. Everyone thought he was in Los Angeles on business for the company."

"Shot?" She still nodded, up and down. "But why?"

"They don't know yet. Robbery, perhaps."

"How awful," she said.

She said it, but her thin face was distracted as if not thinking about Sam Garnet at all. Trying to puzzle out something that had no connection to Sam Garnet. Not really concerned with Garnet, or with something called murder.

"She's a healthy girl, isn't she?" Celia Pearson said. "Jitsuko. Pretty. Alan calls her 'Suko.' " She smiled.

James Pearson went to her, touched her.

"Come down for breakfast," he said.

"Yes," Celia said. "In a little while."

Pearson nodded, left her alone in her room.

*

Harry Wood guided Alice Garnet into The Dregs. A coffee house on the first floor of an old white frame mansion, every inch of its walls were covered with unframed paintings and violent underground slogans. Bearded and paint-stained men and defiant-eyed women lingered over cups of coffee and read books.

Alice Garnet was surprised. "I wouldn't have thought a policeman would come here."

"It's quiet, they let a man alone."

Alice Garnet looked around. "I used to think that the kids were going to abandon art. A useless con game. But it's surprising how many still want to paint or write novels."

"Is that what you do?" Wood asked.

"Sometimes. I could always draw, still try to paint," she said. "I'm an artist in an ad agency, Sergeant. Palmer and Hart, 'We Do It *Your* Way.' That's what I do. You drift into using what talent you have, don't you? Or perhaps a policeman doesn't do that."

"In a way we do, I guess," Wood said.

The waitress came. They ordered plain coffee. When it arrived, Alice Garnet drank hers in silence for a time.

"Can we talk about Sam?" Wood said.

"I don't know much to talk about, Sergeant. You probably know more about Sam than I do. His friends would, anyway." She sipped her coffee. "It's funny, we were close in a way, yet we never got along. Too independent, both of us. We didn't approve of each other, yet loved each other. No other family, you know?"

"Did he tell you about his trip? Where he was going?"

"Los Angeles. He said he'd be at The Carleton Hotel in Hollywood. Perhaps three days, business for Hook Instrument."

"You know what business? Any specific plans?"

"Sam rarely talked to me about Hook Instrument, or anything he did outside Hook."

"What was there outside Hook Instrument?"

"Real estate, buying and selling, stocks. Mainly River Enterprises, I suppose. Sam was the kind of man who always wanted more, just because it was there to get, you know? Any enterprise or deal just because it was around. For the sense of power, I think, as much as anything else."

"Any special project lately?"

"Not that I know."

"Girls?"

"All he could get. I never have understood men like Sam. What's the pleasure in a lot of different women? We're all pretty much the same, aren't we? In bed, anyway."

"In bed, maybe, not out of bed," Wood said. He drank his coffee. "I never saw much to want in a woman a week. I'd like one good one."

"You're not married, Sergeant?"

"No," he said, "I never was."

Wood sensed his voice grow hoarse. He'd gotten it out— he was single, and he wanted a woman. Had he planned it, wanted to tell her? He didn't know. She probably did.

"Any trouble at Hook Instrument?" Wood said.

"He didn't mention any."

"Outside the company? River Enterprises?"

"Anne Thesiger was pushing her husband to stop managing The River Inn again. Anne never did like Sam. It was mutual. Sam said Jim Pearson married a Hook girl and made the company, George Thesiger only made the other Hook girl."

"You ever hear him mention gambling?"

"Only that the house always wins."

"Maybe not always. Losers can get mad. You know that River Enterprises runs a casino in the county?"

"I heard rumors, that's all," she said. "If enough people wanted to gamble, Sam would have given it to them."

"A businessman," Wood said. "Any angle?"

She nodded, finished her coffee. "Who could have killed him, Sergeant? Why?"

"Maybe someone from his past."

"You mean when he was on the police?"

"Possible," Wood said. "Who gets his money, the property, his business interests?"

"I do, I suppose. There's no one else."

"When you saw him yesterday, was there any hint that he wasn't going to L.A.? Any slip about other plans? Was the business trip real at all?"

"I don't remember anything. You better talk to old man Hook, or Jim Pearson."

Before they left the coffee house, Wood called his office to have them check The Carleton Hotel in Hollywood, try to trace Sam Garnet's movements. Then he drove Alice Garnet back to her brother's house for her car.

*

The Thesigers' ranch-style brick house was in a new development on the northern edge of Brandwater. Water poured through the downspouts, and the small house seemed to float on the run-off of the heavy rain. At a living room window, Anne Thesiger lit another cigarette.

"Christ!" she said. "Sam Garnet. Murdered!"

"Don't sound too happy, Anne," George Thesiger said.

People in Brandwater didn't often drink before five o'clock and the ritual cocktail hour, but Thesiger was mixing a drink at the living room bar. A small living room, in precise order, where everything matched in pastel blues. George Thesiger's hands shook as he poured the whisky, his heavy face distracted. He drank, ran his hand through his wavy gray hair.

"What was he doing in a motel like that?" Anne Thesiger said. She turned. "He told you it was a business trip?"

"The police think he might have been meeting a woman. Under a phony name, Vause said."

"When did Sam Garnet hide a woman?"

"A married woman, maybe," Thesiger said, drank.

Anne turned back to the window, looked out at the torrent of January rain. Thesiger watched her for a moment, then looked away, his eyes vacant as if turned inside, thinking. Anne spoke over her shoulder.

"I always said there was something, didn't I? Garnet and Celia. No, you said, impossible, not my delicate sister. But when Celia joined Jim in Japan back there in the Korean War, Sam Garnet was over there, too. When she came home she looked like hell. Half crazy ever since, right?"

"She'd had a bad miscarriage," Thesiger said absently.

"A lot of women have miscarriages. I've had three, and no Alan to make me feel better."

"You're tougher."

"You bet I am," she said, turned and crushed out her cigarette in a pastel blue ashtray. "I wish you were."

"Maybe I'm tougher than you think."

Anne held another cigarette, didn't light it. "What do you mean by that?"

"Nothing. Never mind."

Anne lit the cigarette. "Who gets his money and holdings, George? The sister?"

"Unless he left everything to charity."

"Sam was a real charitable man," Anne said. "His place at Hook Instrument is open. Talk to my father."

"I don't want his place at Hook Instrument," Thesiger said, finished his drink. "I have to go out. Keep the doors locked, someone murdered Sam Garnet."

Anne watched from the window as George Thesiger walked to their garage through the heavy rain.

*

The big Pearson house was three blocks up the hill from Sam Garnet's home, gray and ugly in the rain. The lawn was already sodden, water running off the hard adobe clay underneath. A middle-aged housekeeper answered Harry Wood's ring.

"I'll take it, Frieda," a voice called from inside.

The housekeeper disappeared inside the big, echoing house. Celia Pearson, in a blue cardigan, smiled at Wood.

"Can I help you?"

"I'd like to talk to your husband, Mrs. Pearson."

"Of course. Come in."

Wood stepped into an elegant entry hall with a polished wood floor. Celia Pearson took him into a formal living room with stiff French chairs, wood-and-brocade love seats, period couches and porcelain lamps. She walked with a brisk stride like some long-legged girl.

"I'll get Jim. Would you like some coffee?"

"Thanks, I've already had some."

She nodded, still smiling, and turned to go out of the bleak living room. She stopped. Her thin face was confused. She turned back, looked at Wood as if trying to remember what he had wanted.

"Jim? Why, he's at his office. You know that, Mr.—"

She blinked. "Do I know you?"

"Detective-Sergeant Wood, ma'am. Police. I'll—"

"A policeman?"

"Sam Garnet's murder, Mrs. Pearson."

"Oh, yes," she nodded, agreeable, as if Wood had just told her there would be a ladies' club meeting. "Sam Garnet. He's dead." Another nod, a smile at Wood, and then her thin hand went to her throat, squeezed. "It's Alan! You want Alan! You suspect Alan, don't you? I know that!"

"Why would we do that, Mrs. Pearson?"

She seemed not to hear. "Poor Alan. He's not strong, you see? I knew something would happen."

"They didn't get along? Alan and Sam Garnet?"

"They didn't get along, Alan and Sam Garnet, you see?" she said. "My husband's friend, for a long, long time. We were all together. Alan hates Sam. Something about me, you see? I've tried to protect him, Alan."

"Does your son have a class ring? A blue stone?"

"What? Why, yes, he does. He was valedictorian." Pride.

"Is Alan at home, Mrs. Pearson?"

"Of course. I'll get him."

She walked out of the room. Wood watched her go. The stiff living room was immaculate. The work of servants. Celia Pearson returned alone, her smile more confused now.

"Alan doesn't seem to be at home."

"Where can I find him?"

She shook her head. "You know boys. A secretive age, nineteen. He went off with that girl. She's Japanese. She seems such a sweet girl."

"Does Alan gamble, Mrs. Pearson?"

"Alan? Oh, no, never. He's not really well."

"If you see him, tell him we want to talk to him."

"Yes," Celia Pearson said. "He went out without his raincoat. I hope he's not getting too wet."

Wood went out to his car, the rain even heavier.

4

Wood stopped for a hamburger and a beer, and it was one-thirty before he got back to his desk in the squad room. Detective (Second-Grade) Phil Martin came over.

"I've got the report on Sam Garnet's L.A. trip, Harry."

"Give it to me."

Martin flipped his notebook open. "Vinnie Tugela, that sort of handyman he used to operate his boat and run errands, drove him to the airport. He took the six-fifteen flight out to L.A., checked into The Carleton Hotel in Hollywood at seven-twenty-five. He had dinner at the hotel, was seen around, went bar-hopping on the strip with a guy named Randall, one of Hook Instrument's suppliers. Got back to the hotel about eleven-fifteen, left a call for nine-thirty. He had a ten-thirty A.M. meeting with Randall. Didn't answer the call or make the meeting."

Martin closed his notebook.

"He make any calls, have any visitors in Hollywood?"

"No visitors, no calls from his room."

"Who set up the meeting with this Randall?"

"Garnet did."

"Anything from the lab on the murder scene?"

"Not a thing. No special dirt, dust or any other physical evidence. The car gave us nothing. Fingerprints are all negative so far; the gun was wiped. It'd been oiled recently."

"Evidence of recent sex?"

"Doc says no. Garnet hadn't taken a bath, either."

Wood nodded. Detective Martin went away. Wood sat silent for a time. He was still thinking when Captain Vause called him into the Captain's private office. County Prosecutor Charles Tucker sat with Vause. Tucker was a very tall, youthful man on his way up to bigger things. His office was down in San Vicente, but he looked worried.

"God," Tucker said, "I even did real-estate business with Garnet myself. Poker only yesterday. What could he have been doing in a crummy motel like that?"

"What do you have so far, Harry?" Captain Vause asked.

Wood gave them the report on Sam Garnet's trip, and on his talks with Alice Garnet and Celia Pearson. He told them about the search of Garnet's home office, and about the blue stone.

"Had Alan Pearson been in any trouble with Garnet?" Wood asked Prosecutor Tucker.

"Well, the boy never seemed to like Garnet, seemed to resent him," Tucker said. "But you can't think it was Alan? High-school honor student, top freshman now at Berkeley. A quiet boy, never in trouble. Celia Pearson pampers him, but he's a steady kid."

"Girl?" Wood said. "He brought one home."

"From Berkeley, a Jap exchange student," Captain Vause said. "George Thesiger says there was trouble with Celia Pearson at the airport when they arrived. Garnet was out there, too."

"What's this girl's name?" Wood asked.

"Jitsuko Ikeda."

Wood thought. "That's an expensive house Garnet had. He lived high and wide."

"You sound jealous, Wood," Tucker said.

"Maybe I am. I was new in the department when Garnet left to join Hook Instrument. He started high. Security Chief."

"He was in the army with Jim Pearson in Korea. When they came home, old man Hook used his pull to get Garnet into the department. Then when he needed a security chief, he hired Sam."

"Twelve years to vice-president."

"He was a good businessman," Tucker said.

Wood said, "Captain, how many times were you invited to have a drink in Garnet's house?"

"Not many, Vause said. "Why?"

"But yesterday he invited us both in," Wood said. "Did he usually go to bed early, have people drive him around?"

"No," Vause said. "On both."

"What's on your mind, Wood?" Tucker asked.

"Just this," Wood said. "Garnet set up the L.A. meeting himself. He made a point of telling everyone he was going —even the police. He made sure he was seen in L.A. He pretended to go to bed extra early, left a morning call. What's it sound like?"

"Something happened in L.A., sent him back here," Vause said.

"No," Tucker said. "The whole trip was a cover. He planned to sneak back up here, go to that motel."

"To *do* something," Wood said. "Something important, and that he didn't want known. Secret, and maybe criminal.

He took his gun, used a fake name, went to a cheap motel."

"To meet the killer?" Tucker said. "Lured back up here?"

"That's possible."

"How else would the killer have found him?" Vause said.

"He made one local call from the motel," Wood said. "He let the killer into the room, and I think his gun was on the motel desk in plain sight. He wasn't worried. The killer just grabbed the gun, shot him. Who could surprise him like that, except someone he trusted? Maybe even a friend?"

Vause and Prosecutor Tucker were silent. They shifted in their chairs. Sam Garnet's friends were important people in the county—people Vause and Tucker knew too.

"Garnet had fingers in a lot of pies," Vause said. "Some we probably don't even know. It didn't have to be a friend."

"We'll know that when we know what he came back to do."

Tucker cleared his throat. "Sheriff Hoag and I can give you some help. I'll send my best man, Lee Beckett."

"I don't need help," Wood said. "Do I, Captain?"

"It's your case, Harry, but—?"

"I'll keep you both filled in," Wood said, walked out.

At his desk, Wood sat toying with a pencil. He broke the pencil. There was a lot of money in this, a lot of local power, and someone had killed Sam Garnet. Wood called Phil Martin.

"Phil, contact the people at U. of Cal.–Berkeley, find out all you can about an exchange student named Jitsuko Ikeda. When she came over, why. Check her connection to

Alan Pearson."

Wood got his hat and slicker, went out to his car.

*

The sea was high and gray along the dunes where the freeway from Monteverde reached the coast and turned south. On a hidden beach at the end of a rutted sand road, the wind blew the rain in sheets. After lunch in the Mexican-American town of Hidalgo, Alan Pearson and Jitsuko Ikeda walked the deserted, wind-swept beach with the waves tumbling and crashing.

The girl had to shout. "It makes me think of my home!"

Alan nodded, smiling. He was wrapped in an old beach blanket, the rain dripping from his hair and thin face, fogging his glasses. He didn't try to answer above the noise of the waves, and his smile was small. The Japanese girl wore a raincoat and beret, strode out, enjoying the wind and rain.

"People forget that we Japanese are a sea people," she said against the wind. "Where I come from, once everyone was a fisherman. There was nothing else they would do."

Alan shouted, "I'm glad you decided to give up fishing."

"Too dirty and smelly!" Jitsuko laughed.

Alan pointed to a sheltered barranca in the beach cliffs, and they ran for it. Its sides protected them from the wind-driven rain, there was an overhang, and from the open mouth they could see the violent sea breaking high and foaming on the beach. Alan held the small girl, kissed her. She pushed him away, smiled.

"We are too wet, Alan," Jitsuko said.

Alan sat down on a rock, looked out at the angry sea. "Sam Garnet was shot last night, Suko. Murdered."

"Murder?" she said. "At his house?"

"No, at some motel," Alan said. He looked at her. "What made you say that? About his house?"

"No reason, Alan." She picked up a stone. "A guess."

He watched her throw the stone. "It could mean trouble. Maybe I better take you back to Berkeley, Suko."

"You mean trouble for your family?"

"Maybe. Garnet was pretty close to my parents."

"I will stay with you," Jitsuko said. "Why was he killed?"

"No one seems to know. He was supposed to be in Los Angeles on a business trip for the company. He sneaked back with some fake name, took a room at a cheap motel, had a gun."

Jitsuko crouched down, traced a circle in the sand. "When did this happen, Alan?"

"I'm not sure. About two in the morning, I think."

"After you left me in the cottage?"

"Yes, maybe an hour later."

She went on drawing circles in the sand. "You did not like Mr. Garnet, did you? At the airport, I saw that."

"He was always around us. All my life. I don't know why Mother and Dad liked him. Coarse and rough, a cop. He left the police, but he was still a cop, really. I could see him using my father, too damned familiar with my mother."

"Familiar? You mean, perhaps, more than a friend?"

"My Aunt Anne used to hint at it," Alan said bitterly.

"At the airport, when your mother was . . . sick? Mr. Garnet was there, too."

"I know," Alan said.

"You love your mother very much, yes?"

"She's always tried to protect me as if I were the sick one. But she's sick, and I think it started when I was born.

31

She was in a sanitarium a long time then, my Aunt Anne told me. I guess I feel she got sick because of me, and—" He stopped, looked at the girl who stood up now, brushed her hands.

"You went driving after you left me last night, Alan."

"I couldn't sleep, drove around for a while."

"Until two-thirty. I saw you come back."

"You don't think it was me who—?"

"No, Alan. I know you, I think. But the police?"

"Let them ask! All I did was drive. They won't find anything."

"But we will not talk about last night."

Alan nodded moodily. Then he looked up. "Suko? If you saw me come back, you were still up too."

She smiled down. "I could not sleep, either."

*

Hook Instrument Company was a group of three large, almost windowless industrial buildings and an office building on the bank of the Santa Rosa River in the slums. The river was already swollen and running high in the rain.

In the office, Wood asked for James Pearson.

"Second floor, Sergeant. End of the corridor, left."

Pearson's outer office was all business. Metal-and-leather furniture, framed pictures of industrial instruments on plain white walls. A working office, without frills.

"Go right in, Sergeant," the secretary said.

James Pearson stood up behind his desk. The tall executive wore a gray suit with a new black armband. There was an efficient strength to the spartan office, but Pearson's blue eyes were vague, something ineffectual to his movements as he waved Wood to a chair. A fog of shock in his eyes, the full mouth pinched, his nose standing out as if the rest of his face had shrunk.

"It's about Sam Garnet, isn't it?" Pearson said.

"Can you tell me anything, Mr. Pearson?"

"No, I can't tell you anything." Pearson sat down, looked down at his soft hands. "Sam was our best executive."

"You knew him very well?"

"Almost twenty-five years." Pearson breathed deeply. "Then, no one knows everything about a man—except perhaps his woman, the real woman." He looked up. "You're sure it wasn't robbery?"

"It's always possible."

Pearson half-smiled. "Your judgment's against it, though."

"He'd come back under cover for some reason. He had his gun. Made a phone call, had five hundred in cash on him," Wood said. "Was his L.A. trip legitimate? You approved it?"

"Yes. He arranged it, but I'd wanted it for some time."

"Any trouble in your company? Some reason for his return in secret?"

"None, Sergeant. Sam was ready for promotion to executive vice-president, in fact," Pearson said. An opaque mist seemed to cover his eyes, seeing distance and time. "Sam came into the company on influence, largely mine, but he more than justified it. We were old buddies, you know? A strange combination, I suppose."

His voice seemed to ramble, rummage in time. "Opposites, eh? Maybe that's the best team. Sam was action, I tend to be thought. He never hesitated, I always did. Cornelius Hook to oversee both of us. It worked well most of the time."

Wood listened to the tall executive. Pearson was rambling through his life, seeing the years. Close death can do that.

"But he had no reason to sneak back here for Hook Instrument?"

Pearson shook his head as if trying to understand. "He had many other business interests, though. Moonlighting, I suppose you call it. Inevitable for an ambitious man in a small community. You have money and power, you use that to get more. People want your power, do you favors. Sam had many ventures."

"River Enterprises?"

"Mostly through River, yes. Owned The River Inn, apartments, gas stations, an office building, even a gambling casino."

"You gamble, Mr. Pearson?"

He shook his head.

"How was River Enterprises organized?"

"Private corporation. Forty percent owned by Sam, thirty by George Thesiger, thirty by silent partners."

"Alice Garnet gets Sam's forty percent?"

"I suppose so." His sigh was tired. "Alice will sell it, she won't want Sam's business. Not her way."

"Who takes his place in your company?"

"We haven't thought about that." His half-smile was almost neutral. "My sister-in-law will want it for George Thesiger. She'll badger her father, a determined woman. But he has no experience in our line, won't want it anyway."

"How did Thesiger and Garnet get along?"

"Well enough. Sam didn't think too much of George's ability, and Anne didn't like Sam. Because of Sam's opinion, I suppose."

"You're sure she didn't like Garnet? Not an act? He

might have sneaked back to that motel to meet a woman."

"Anne?" A new idea to him? "She often accused Sam of being a lecher, even—" Pearson stopped. "I don't know, I doubt it."

"Your wife had some trouble at the airport yesterday? A shock? Sam Garnet was out there?"

"My wife is . . . nervous. The excitement was too much."

"What excitement? Your son and a girl?"

"The noise, the crowd. She hates crowds."

"I hear your son resented Sam Garnet, too close to you."

"Alan?" The fog in Pearson's eyes. "No, not really."

"You know where Alan is?"

"At home, I suppose."

"I went there. Your wife said he was out with the girl."

"My wife?" Pearson stood up. "You talked to Celia? Was she . . . all right? What did you say to her?"

"I asked for you and Alan. She seemed okay. Shouldn't she?"

Pearson sat down. "Yes, most of the time she's normal. She has spells, Sergeant. Breakdowns. Not for a long time, but she's been in sanitariums."

"What started these spells, Mr. Pearson?"

Pearson shook his head. "A private matter. A miscarriage. A long time ago. I'd thought it was—" he trailed off.

"Nothing to do with Sam Garnet? I'm sorry, I have to ask."

"No, nothing to do with Sam."

Wood got up. "Thanks, Mr. Pearson."

"Yes," Pearson said, nodded, looked up. "You don't expect this, do you? It doesn't happen. Tragedy in your own life."

Wood left the tall executive watching one of his walls.

5

James Pearson watched from his office window as Sergeant Wood drove off through the steady rain. He looked for a moment at the rising Santa Rosa River, as if trying to decide if there was something he should do, then turned to his intercom, told his secretary he was going home for the day, and left.

When he reached his big house on its hill, the rain was flowing down the driveway, and Alan's Porsche was there.

In the dark living room, Celia was busily using a spray can of polish on the old French furniture. She hummed to herself as she sprayed and rubbed in the bleak light.

"Are you all right, Celia?" Pearson asked.

She polished. "Why, what are you doing home, dear?"

"The police talked to you? About Sam Garnet?"

"He's dead. Poor Sam." She went on polishing, the light so dim no shine showed.

James Pearson watched her as if aware of something about her she didn't know herself. He left her humming and polishing, and went up to his son's room on the second floor. His movements were like a man who steps carefully in a dark night. Alan and Jitsuko Ikeda were looking through Alan's high school scrapbook.

"Can I ask you where you were last night, Alan?" James Pearson said. "Jitsuko, too?"

"She was in the cottage," Alan said. "I was in bed."

"You're sure, son? I have to know."

"I'm sure."

James Pearson nodded. "All right. I'm sorry I disturbed—"

"Dad?" Alan said. "As long as I can remember, Sam Garnet was around the house. He acted like it was *his* house."

"My friend and vice-president, Alan."

"Your friend, or mother's friend?"

Pearson smiled. "Don't listen to your Aunt Anne too much. She didn't like Sam Garnet, she's jealous of your mother."

"Mother owns the company stock, right? Mother, Grandfather Hook, and Aunt Anne. Not you."

"I vote it, Alan. Your grandfather and I run the company."

Alan said, "What's been wrong with Mother all these years, Dad? Why is she always so . . . nervous?"

"She was never strong, and later she found a child difficult. We're sorry for that, unfair to you. Parents are human."

"Was Sam Garnet part of what's been wrong?" Alan said.

"No," Pearson said. He turned to the girl. "Where is your home in Japan, Miss Ikeda?"

"In Sakai, a suburb of Osaka. You have been to Japan?"

"During the Korean War. A special base on Kyushu. My firm does business there, too. Your family is in Sakai?"

"I have no family, Mr. Pearson."

"I see. Well, enjoy yourselves."

Pearson went down to the library. In the living room his wife still polished furniture in the half-dark. Pearson made a drink, sat down, drank in the library without turning on a light.

*

Harry Wood rang the bell of the Thesigers' house in Brandwater. There was no answer, and no cars in the garage. He drove on in the rain to The River Inn. George Thesiger wasn't at the almost deserted roadhouse. The headwaiter didn't know where Thesiger was. Wood asked for Vinnie Tugela's address. It was a rural address on the southwest outskirts of Monteverde.

Wood found the dirt road, and his car skidded in the slick adobe-mud as he drove up the eroded barranca. At the head of the barranca, the old farmhouse looked abandoned, but a green sportscar was parked at the side. When he got out, Wood saw movement on the screened porch. As he sloshed up through the rain, a girl came out onto the steps.

"If you want Vinnie, he isn't here."

She was tall, with full breasts and good hips. Her face was high-boned, her long hair blonde. She wore a green pants suit, and tossed her hair to show it off. Theatrical. But too much—the local beauty who wanted more, but who was getting older.

"Where is Tugela?"

"The boat, I guess. He got a call, said he was going."

"What boat is that?"

"Sam Garnet's boat down at Cuyama Beach. Not that Sam's going to need it or me. I guess Vinnie figures he can have both now. I'm supposed to wait here." She eyed Wood up and down.

"Will you, Miss—?"

"Virginia Gallo. You have some better idea?"

"You knew Sam Garnet pretty well?"

Her face closed. "You better talk to Vinnie."

"When did you see Sam Garnet last?"

"What are you? A cop?"

"Detective-Sergeant Harry Wood."

"Look, I don't know anything about what happened to Sam!"

She turned and went back into the house. Wood stood for a moment in the rain. Then he went back to his car. He drove carefully down the muddy side road to the county highway, and then to the freeway and south toward Fremont and Cuyama Beach.

Fremont, the third city of Buena Costa County, is on the coast southwest of Monteverde. A grimy town of fishing, canneries, fertilizer factories, refineries and chemical plants. Wood passed it, and went on the few miles farther south to Cuyama Beach—a small, elegant village of beach clubs, fenced beaches, Spanish-style villas on terraced hills, and a plush boat marina. The marina gate was locked. Wood blew his horn. A uniformed man came out of the rambling clubhouse, ran up through the rain.

"Harry! What's up?"

"Where do I find Sam Garnet's boat, Walt?"

"Third dock down, last slip. The *Sea King II*."

"Vinnie Tugela aboard?"

"I don't know. He's got a key, uses the side gate. Too bad about Sam Garnet."

Wood drove through the gate to the parking lot. He

walked to the third dock in the windy rain. The sea pounded the marina sea wall, storm signals were flying, no boats were out. The *Sea King II* strained at its hawsers, its rope fenders out. Wood saw no one on deck, climbed aboard the cabin cruiser.

The hatchway down to the main cabin was open despite the storm. Wood went down. No one was there. Why was the cabin open if no one was aboard? He looked into the narrow forward sleeping cabin. It was empty, but a small door was open at the far end. Wood peered through the open door into a shallow storage locker.

He sensed the shadow and movement behind him.

A driving shoulder caught him in the back, flung him on his face into the storage locker. Wood struggled up, hit his head on the low ceiling, and the door clanged shut.

Footsteps hurried away outside.

Swearing, Wood pushed at the small door. It was metal, solid, and there was no room to move in the cramped locker.

Wood began to shout in the noise of the storm.

*

Anne Thesiger watched the rain sweep across the golf course of The Monteverde Country Club. At the bar she ordered another highball, listened to the strange undercurrent of distant sound in the quiet lounge—the Santa Rosa River flowing fast.

Anne couldn't remember when she'd heard the river last. Perhaps once when she was a girl. In the good days before Jim Pearson married Celia and left George Thesiger for her. When she'd been her father's favorite, Celia too prim and proper for the rough old man. When she had known the company would be hers, the envied queen of Monteverde.

Before Jim Pearson and Sam Garnet.

She had had to marry a glad-hander who didn't like to get up early or work steadily. Then, he was an easy man to live with. She liked George because he was soft and easy-going—and hated him because he was soft and easy-going. She sighed, drank, and saw George come into the lounge. He sat beside her.

"River's running way up," George said.

He nodded to the bartender for a whisky.

"Where've you been?"

"Working." He grinned at her, his eyes alive.

"I talked to my father. You could handle Personnel."

"Stop talking to him."

"No! I want us to have what belongs to me!"

"I've got other plans."

"You'll be a vice-president, damn it!"

"No I won't," George Thesiger said, drank.

*

Harry Wood had been shouting for an hour, the wind and rain outside covering his cries. He cursed silently, there was nothing in the cramped locker to use on the metal door. He sat and listened to the violent creaking of the boat, and heard a different sound. Someone was out in the cabin. Wood shouted:

"Hey! In the locker!"

The movement outside stopped, then came closer. The door was unlocked, swung open, and a face peered in. A young, lazy face with a thick mustache under long hair.

"What you doing in there, Sergeant?" Vinnie Tugela said.

Wood climbed out, brushed his suit. "You don't know?"

"Just got back. Thirsty, you know? You can check the bar."

Tugela lounged against the galley sink, his tall, athletic body loose in his heavy sweater and corduroy pants. Confident, he had an alibi, his wind-wrinkled eyes smiling at Wood.

"Who else would be on the boat? The cabin was open."

"I guess I left it open. Maybe Sam Garnet's ghost was here."

The big roustabout laughed.

"You got a phone call to come down. From a ghost?"

"Some guy was worried the storm'd damage the boat. Don't know who it was. Got to take care of the boat."

"Sam Garnet left it to you?"

"Sure like that, only it belongs to River Enterprises. Mr. Garnet liked things in the company name. Taxes, I guess."

"Alice Garnet gets Sam's share?"

"I guess so."

"But she won't run River. Who will? George Thesiger?"

"I wouldn't know, Sergeant. I just work here."

"Doing what, besides running the boat?"

"This and that. Whatever Mr. Garnet wanted."

"You work at the gambling casino?"

"What casino?" Tugela said.

Wood held up the black hundred-dollar plaque. "This casino."

"Hell, that could come from anywhere."

Tugela moved away from the galley sink. He picked up a yellow slicker-jacket, took out a pack of cigarettes. He lit one, eyed the black plaque in Wood's hand. Wood pocketed the plaque again.

"Where'd you find that?" Vinnie Tugela said.

"In the room where Sam Garnet was shot."

Tugela smoked. The boat groaned and creaked in the storm.

"Nice girl, that Virginia Gallo," Wood said. "One of Sam Garnet's women, right? But at your house now."

"At my house before," Tugela said. "She needs a younger guy, you know?"

"How come you drove Garnet to the airport last evening?"

"He told me to."

"The trip to L.A. was a phony, a cover. He had a fake driver's license ready. What was he going to do back here?"

"He didn't even tell me he was coming back."

Wood said, "He was hiding, had his gun, wanted a good alibi. Some big trouble, Tugela, a danger to him, I think. You don't have any idea what it was?"

"No."

"He made one local call. Where were you last night?"

"Home, after eleven. He didn't call me."

"Why would you lie? Stay around town, though. Okay?"

Wood went to the gangway up, and saw the glasses on the galley counter. Two glasses, both half full of more than water. Two men had been there. He turned back toward Tugela.

"You know," Tugela said, "with Sam Garnet dead, there's a lot of money loose around the county. With luck, we can all get some of it."

"Who was here with you?" Wood said.

"No one. I wasn't here," Tugela said. "A lot of money, Sergeant. Maybe you could get your share."

Wood stepped closer, hit Tugela with the back of his

hand. The big boat-handler didn't give a step, or hit back. He stood solid in the rocking boat, not smiling and not moving. Wood turned for the gangway again, went up into the rain and off the boat. Tugela was the stronger man, but he was a cop. It didn't make him feel especially clean.

*

Wood stopped in Fremont for some beers and dinner. Someone had been on the boat with Vinnie Tugela—someone who didn't want to be seen there. Who and why?

It was after eight when he got back to the squad room. The night men were all talking about the rain, Captain Vause had gone, and Wood was tired. No word from Phil Martin on the Ikeda girl. The duty sergeant had a report on Sam Garnet's rented car.

"Reserved by phone from L.A. International, used the Tracy name. He picked it up at eleven-thirty, paid cash in advance, said he'd leave it in Burbank."

Aside from the manager, the maid, and Sam Garnet, the fingerprints were all unidentified. Diaz's lab report was complete, and negative. The motel manager had checked out clean.

Wood filled out his day-report, and at ten o'clock got his hat and went home. He lived alone in a cottage that had been his father's until the old man died a few years ago. It was near a creek, and Wood stood at a window and watched the torrent.

He got a beer, and watched television. He thought about Vinnie Tugela and money, and about the Gallo girl. Tugela was getting more than money from Sam Garnet's death. That made Wood think about Alice Garnet. He hung his suit on a chair, went to bed. He didn't go to sleep.

His bedroom was small and bare and dull. A cheap room. He hadn't changed anything since his father died. A cold cottage, lonely. Nothing like Sam Garnet's lush bachelor playground.

Wood didn't sleep well.

6

Harry Wood awoke to gray light and the steady sound of the rain. He sat up on the edge of his bed, lit a cigarette. The rumble of the creek filled the cottage. He liked the sound, clean and alive. On sunny days the cottage was bright and pleasant. It was paid for, and he had his work. He began to dress.

Before he left, he called his office. There was no news. Wood stopped on the road for some eggs and coffee, then drove to the Thesigers' house. The ranch-style brick house was like an island in the rain. Anne Thesiger answered the door.

"Yes? What is it?"

Impatient and irritable, the narrow-faced blonde wore a red robe and carried a cup of coffee.

"Sergeant Wood, Mrs. Thesiger. Can I talk to you?"

"Come in, then."

Wood followed Anne Thesiger through a pastel-blue living room into the kitchen. George Thesiger sat in a breakfast nook.

"Sergeant Wood, George," Anne Thesiger introduced.

George Thesiger stood up, held out his hand. He smiled

his gregarious real-estate man's smile. Wood shook hands. Thesiger was nervous, tight, and his hand sweated.

"Terrible about Sam," Thesiger said. "Any leads yet?"

"Some. How were things at River Enterprises, Mr. Thesiger?"

"Never better. Poor Sam."

"You got along? No problems?"

"We worked together. No troubles I know about."

"But you weren't friends?"

Anne Thesiger said, "You mean me, right? Everyone knows I didn't like how George was treated, a saloonkeeper. He should never have been Sam Garnet's partner anyway, he should have had Garnet's position at Hook Instrument. Maybe Jim Pearson's position. I'm the older sister."

"Jim developed the electronic valve," George Thesiger said. "Jesus, Anne, he doubled your father's business. He's good."

"You're not good?" Anne snapped.

"At other things, damn it! Not valves and crummy meters!"

"What other things, George?"

"You'll find out."

"When, George?"

Her voice was cutting, petulant. Wood saw the kind of woman she was. Everything except what she wanted at any moment was boring, an inconvenience. The necessities of life were inconvenient. The needs of others were inconvenient. It was unfair that there were things she had to do when she didn't feel like it. Any requirement was an unfair annoyance. In the end, life was something of an imposition.

"Where were you both two nights ago? Late?" Wood said.

"Us?" Anne said, amazed.

"We're pretty sure Garnet knew the killer," Wood said.

"Now you listen, Sergeant. My father—" Anne began.

George Thesiger said, "I was here at home. All night. Anne was in San Vicente at an art show."

"Until two A.M.?"

"An opening, Sergeant," a sneer in her voice, saying that a policeman wouldn't know about such things. "A big party afterwards. I was there until almost two. I often stay with an old girl friend, Mrs. Glenda Forbes, when I'm late in San Vicente. But I was tired, drove home, got here about three A.M."

"Who saw you there, Mrs. Thesiger?"

"Glenda Forbes for one, and the gallery director, Peter Eyk."

Wood made a note of the names.

"So you were alone all night, Mr. Thesiger?" Wood said.

"Yes."

Wood closed his notebook. "What can you tell me about Sam Garnet's women?"

"He never seemed to have any problems, if that's what you're thinking," George Thesiger said.

"No special woman?"

Anne Thesiger snorted. "A revolving door."

"Was Virginia Gallo one of his women?"

"I guess so," Thesiger said. "She moved around."

"To Vinnie Tugela, too?"

"Tugela? No. I mean, it's news to me."

48

"Any married women, Mr. Thesiger?"

George Thesiger drank his coffee. "I don't suppose Garnet would have missed a chance."

"I know one woman he had a problem with," Anne Thesiger said. "His sister. Ironic, eh? Now she gets all he had. I wonder where she was at two A.M. that night?"

"Shut up!" George Thesiger said. His coffee slopped. He steadied the cup with both hands.

"What kind of problems did Sam and the sister have?"

Thesiger said, "They just had different ways of living."

"Mrs. Thesiger?" Wood said.

She shrugged. "Nothing specific."

"Neither of you know what Garnet was going to do back up here that night?"

They shook their heads. Anne Thesiger lit a cigarette, folded her arms. She was watching Thesiger as Wood left.

*

Cornelius Hook was sixty-nine. A broad, heavy old man whose solid torso was longer than his thick legs. His hair was gray, not yet white, and he had the vigor and stubborn endurance of his South African *voortrekker* ancestors who, at his age, lived a week in the saddle and destroyed fifteen thousand Zulus at the end of the week. Unlike them, he had no beard, and wore expensive suits. His eyes were clear blue, and, like the *voortrekkers*, he knew the world he lived in.

Hook was alone at breakfast in his formal dining room when James Pearson came in and sat down. A Mexican houseman brought another cup of coffee. Hook watched his son-in-law and president like some monolithic old owl in his high-backed chair. James Pearson rubbed at his face and eyes with both hands.

"You look tired," Hook said.

"Yes," Pearson said. "The river's rising at the plant." He closed his eyes. "I'm worried about Celia."

"Worse?"

"Too busy. Polishing, dusting, humming all day. She's forgotten we've got a housekeeper and two cleaning women. Back in the past again. Too happy."

"It's a sign," Hook said. "You've headed it off before."

"I have to run the company. With Sam dead—" Pearson looked at his watch. "Ten-thirty, and I'm just going in."

"We need a new vice-president."

Pearson was silent. For nearly a minute. "You're a cold man, Cornelius. I never really saw that before. You don't work for the reward, for comfort and security. Just to have more, the bigger man. Don't you think we should bury Sam first?"

"I like matters settled. Anne is on me about George Thesiger. It would be nice to get her off me for my old age. Could George do the job?"

"Give it to him," Pearson said. He leaned back and looked up at the beamed ceiling as if interested in the beams, counting them, fascinated. "It can't hurt anyone. Make Anne happy."

The old man watched Pearson, pushed his cup away.

"You always said George was a straw man, useless."

"He won't take the job anyway, Cornelius. He understands that much about himself. I can admire that in him."

Pearson frowned at the ceiling as if something was wrong. The ceiling not what it should be, too many or too few beams, not proper. He counted the beams again, his lips moving.

"What did it?" Hook said. "To Celia this time? Alan, the girl, Sam Garnet's murder?"

"All three, I suppose." Pearson counted the beams once more, shook his head as if not satisfied. He looked at Hook. "I don't know if I can help her enough any more, Cornelius. Someday she'll have to be alone, on her own."

"Can she be, Jim?"

"I don't know," Pearson said. "Perhaps not."

"Have the police any suspects?" Hook said, patted his suit for his cigars.

"I expect they do by now. They won't tell us, will they?" Pearson looked up at the beams again, shook his head and brought his eyes down. "They're talking of women, a woman. Interested in River Enterprises, and in that fake driver's license Sam had. Illegal connections. They've asked about Alan, too."

"Alan? Why?"

"I'm not sure," Pearson said slowly. "Some idea that Alan suspected Celia and Sam of a relation."

"Anne and her stupid jealousies!" Hook fumed.

"No, not only Anne. I expect it's looked odd to many people. The way our lives worked out. Servants talk, people see."

"Other men have delicate wives," Hook said. "I did, but no one started rumors."

"The police talked to her," Pearson said.

"Celia?" Hook sat forward, smoked.

"A Sergeant Wood. I've seen him with Vause. A quiet man, methodical. He listens, I think, and hears."

"What did he hear from Celia, Jim?"

"Nothing, really. What could she say that would interest the police?"

"No, I suppose not," Hook said, sat back. "What was Sam up to, Jim? Do you know?"

"No."

Pearson got up, stood there and looked at the door.

"Jim? Just take care of Celia. I'll come down to the office if you need help."

James Pearson nodded.

*

Alice Garnet lived in a garden apartment not far from the coffee house where Wood had first talked with her. A rear unit on the ground floor. As Wood reached the door through the puddles, he heard the low, steady rumble.

Alice Garnet opened her door. She listened, too.

"It's the river," she said.

Wood had never heard the sound before.

"You're getting wet," Alice Garnet said.

Wood went into a small apartment cluttered with paintings and drawings. A drawing table with work on it stood beside a table set for a solitary breakfast. There were two small rooms and a kitchenette, the bed unmade in the second room. Pleasant.

"Any news, Sergeant?"

He told her about the report of Sam Garnet's actions in Los Angeles, and about the attack on the boat.

"Someone didn't want me to see him, or her, with Tugela."

She started to clear away her breakfast dishes. "Sam had some plan, didn't he? Something he didn't want known."

"I'd say so," Wood said.

"You think it was criminal, illegal, or worse. But why?

With all Sam had, his position, his power?"

"Maybe to keep it all," Wood said.

"The past? When he was a policeman?"

"Policemen can get mixed in things. Maybe he never stopped."

She carried her dishes into the tiny kitchenette, ran the water in the sink, put them in one at a time. She came back out drying her hands. She sat down. Her dark copper hair was loose. In her stained painting smock her legs looked even better than in a short skirt. Because she was happier in the stained smock.

"Was Virginia Gallo Sam's woman? One of them?"

"I don't know his women. I didn't want to."

"You know Vinnie Tugela?"

She smiled. "The devil-may-care boat bum? Young buck? Only Tugela isn't either of those. Oh, part of him is, but part is also a thirty-plus opportunist with a steel-trap mind."

"What was his relation to Sam?"

"Man Friday and protégé, friend and faithful dog," Alice said. "Some men are odd with their less important friends. One moment pals, the next—go get coffee, boy. Equals man-to-man, but always clear who's the bigger man. Two of a kind, but no doubt left who was better, the boss. I've seen others like that. Old Cornelius Hook for one."

"Would they compete for a woman?"

"Probably. Tugela even made a pass at me, but I laughed at him, and that froze it. Big egos are sensitive."

"Some people seem to think there was something between Sam and Celia Pearson. At one time, anyway."

"Sam and Jim Pearson were close for over twenty years, friends." She smoothed her smock over her thighs. "I've heard that rumor before, though. Mostly Anne Thesiger's work, and I doubt it. Celia had the better man. A nicer man."

"What about Anne Thesiger?"

"You mean Anne and Sam? Good God!" She was silent for a moment. "You mean her hate was a ruse? Or love-hate? She hated Sam for George, but was attracted to him too?"

"It's happened before."

"Anne likes strong men."

Wood said, "She says you and Sam had problems, wonders where you were when Sam was shot."

Alice laughed. "I don't want what Anne wants from life, so of course she doesn't like me. I wouldn't let Sam help me. For Sam, you did what he told you to do, or no help."

"Where were you when he was shot?"

"Here, working on my late-night art. No alibi."

Her eyes didn't evade, neither annoyed nor uneasy. A woman who had seen a lot, controlled, and yet somehow young.

"Taking time off from your job?" Wood said.

"I sell work, not time. I make my own hours."

"What are you going to do with Sam's holdings?"

"I haven't given it much thought yet."

Wood thought. "George Thesiger is jumpy, wound tight. Something on his mind. Who owns the last thirty percent of River Enterprises?"

"Sam never said. Silent partners, you know? Anonymous. His important friends, probably. But Sam ran the company for them, that's why he was the senior partner, not Thesiger."

"Yeh," Wood said. "Important people."

He went to the door.

"Sergeant?" Alice said. "Visit me again."

7

Celia Pearson answered the door of the big Brandwater house. She was all in black, elegant, with gloves, a veil, and a single strand of diamonds at her throat. Dressed to go out.

"You're . . . Sergeant Wood? My husband is at the office. There may be a flood, I hear. He's terribly worried."

"I'd like to see your son, Mrs. Pearson."

"Alan? He's out with the girl Jitsuko. A nice name, isn't it? They went swimming. She has a lovely body."

"Swimming?" Wood said.

Celia Pearson looked up at the sky as if surprised.

"They love the sea, the Japanese." She held her gloved hand out in the rain. "Not the sea, of course, you must think I'm foolish. The indoor pool at the club. It's raining."

She smiled at Wood, began to take off her gloves, and walked away into her house. Wood reached out and closed the door, went back to his car. He drove to the country club on the eastern edge of Brandwater.

An exclusive club, larger than most, because Monteverde was a hot, dusty inland city of middle-class recreations, and there was nowhere for the rich to play in privacy except the club. It had its golf course, tennis courts, pool tables for the older men, card rooms, and two pools—one indoors and one outdoors. The outdoor pool was wind-blown in the rain. A groomed assistant manager conducted Wood to the indoor pool.

Under the high, echoing dome, three people splashed in the thick indoor heat. A few others rested in padded lounge chairs around the edge. They had drinks and food, and one fat older man wore his glasses and worked on some papers. Alan Pearson sat in a chair in Olympic-style bathing trunks, his lean body more muscled than it looked in clothes. Jitsuko Ikeda swung her feet in the water at the side of the pool near Alan.

"You're a cop, right?" Alan Pearson said.

"Sergeant Harry Wood."

"You want to know where I was? Did I murder Sam Garnet."

"Where were you?"

Jitsuko Ikeda slid into the pool, swam away with powerful strokes, at ease in the water.

"I was at home, in bed," Alan Pearson said. "Jitsuko was in our guest cottage. In bed, too. Alone. Okay?"

"If you weren't, would you tell me?" Wood said. He looked at the Japanese girl swimming. "Where did you meet Miss Ikeda?"

"In one of my classes," Alan said. "Why do you ask questions if you know you won't get honest answers?"

"People make mistakes, try too hard. We pick up discrepancies, changes in stories. Lying takes practice. You never know what they'll say if you get them talking," Wood said. "Just in one class? Love at first sight?"

"Science club, too. Mutual friends. Why?"

"I wondered how long you'd known her."

"Long enough. She didn't know Sam Garnet."

"Your high-school ring has a blue stone in it, right? Like this?" Wood held the small stone in his hand. "We found it in Sam Garnet's house, in the office. Someone searched the office."

Alan Pearson said, "I lost my ring. I could have dropped it in Mr. Garnet's house."

"The whole ring, or just the stone?"

"The whole ring."

"But not two nights ago, you were in bed," Wood said.

"I lost it months ago."

"Visiting your friend Sam Garnet?"

"He wasn't my friend. I didn't like him."

"Around your parents too much?"

"That's right. I feel like a swim, okay?"

"Have fun," Wood said.

*

Alan Pearson watched Wood walk around the pool and out. The boy dove into the pool, swam around with his eyes on the entrance. Wood did not come back. Alan waited for Jitsuko to swim past him on one of her steady, tireless lengths.

"Suko? Come on out."

She trod water. "I will do six more lengths."

"Later," Alan said.

He swam to the edge and climbed out. Jitsuko swam in a circle for a moment, then slowly followed him. She picked up a towel. Drying herself, she sat near Alan.

"He was a policeman?" she said. "What did he want?"

"He wanted to know where we were when Garnet was shot."

"What did you tell him, Alan?"

"The same as I told my father," Alan said. "He wanted to know where I met you. How long I've known you."

"Sometimes I think of that." She smiled. "Only a month, but it seems so much longer."

She went on smiling, drying herself briskly, rubbing her smooth, firm young body.

"Why did he ask, Suko?"

Her voice was curt. "It is his job."

"Suko? How did we meet? I mean, you did just happen to take that class with me? Join the science club?"

"We met, yes?" She leaned and kissed his cheek, touched his shoulder. "I was very lucky."

Alan held her, his hands tight on her arms. "How did you know Eddie DeJohn?"

"You know him, Alan. Any pretty girl."

"Sure, I know Eddie," Alan said. "Suko? Where's my class ring? The ring I gave you? You're not wearing it."

She looked at her hand. "Oh, I'm sorry. Stupid, I must have left it in Berkeley."

"Didn't I see you wearing it on the plane?"

"No, you did not see it."

Alan watched her. "The police found a stone like the one in my ring in Sam Garnet's house. His house was searched."

"There must be many such rings in this city," Jitsuko said. She moved closer to him again. "We will not talk about these things that do not matter to us. It is not our concern. We will be together."

She kissed him, smiled up. He put his arms around her in the corner of the hot, echoing indoor space.

✢

The Mexican houseman ushered Harry Wood into Cornelius Hook's library. An open fire burned in the fireplace, and the noise of the brimming Vaal Creek below the house was clean and alive. Cornelius Hook was studying some documents in the front of the open fire. The burly old man looked up at Wood.

"I know you. Wood, right? Police lieutenant?"

"Sergeant, Mr. Hook."

"Ah? I'm sorry. Sergeant, then." The old man put his papers aside. "Any result yet? You *are* here about Sam Garnet?"

"Any thoughts about why Garnet was back here, Mr. Hook?"

"None at all. Like everyone else, I thought he was in L.A." Hook shook his head. "Sam was always engaged in something. Business or personal. At first I was unhappy about his outside interests, but it never hurt his work. The best executive we had at Hook Instrument, not afraid of decisions." The old man smiled. "Next to Jim Pearson and myself, of course."

"You think it was outside trouble? Not Hook Instrument?"

"People don't murder over valves and meters, Sergeant."

"People murder over anything, Mr. Hook," Wood said. "Did you know about some outside trouble Garnet had?"

"No. Sam wasn't a talker; he acted."

"What about his past? When he was a cop?"

"You policemen don't always make friends. Sam was hard."

"Twelve years is a long time, though," Wood said.

"It is."

"Maybe some personal mess?"

"That's about all that's left, isn't it?"

Wood said, "Where were you that night, Mr. Hook?"

"So? Jim Pearson said you were a thorough man. I like that. How long have you been a policeman?"

"Fourteen years."

"And still a sergeant? Too bad. Promotion is slow in a small city, I expect. Not much chance to shine. Routine work."

"Mostly routine," Wood agreed, waited.

"The point, eh? As it happens, I can say where I was. Prosecutor Tucker and I were here talking business. He left about two-fifteen. My houseman saw us part, and I had some supper before I went to bed. Old men don't need much sleep."

"Outside business with Tucker?"

"Yes. In a business community everyone puts his money to use. I expect even you have investments locally."

"No, I don't," Wood said.

"You should do something about that. Get some capital."

"Your daughter and Sam Garnet were close friends, right?" Wood said. "If she didn't like her son's girl, would she have involved Garnet in trying to stop a relation?"

"That incident at the airport? Celia's inclined to think of Alan as a child, overprotective. She excites easily, I'm afraid." Hook frowned. "You're not accusing Alan?"

"Seems he didn't like Garnet much."

"Too coarse, rough. But the English have a proverb, Sergeant: the first generation makes the money; the second goes into politics; the third is a dilettante. Alan is our third generation, he's not capable of violence." Old Hook smiled. "It's all relative, though. My father was a real man. Left South Africa because no one was going to rule him, especially no *Uitlander*. Plowed his own fields, slept with his rifle beside the bed."

"A tough man."

"He was," Hook said, stared at his fire. "Heredity is a chance matter. The Japanese have a good method—adopt good sons, give them the family name. In a way, I did that with Jim Pearson."

"You know Japan well?"

Hook went on watching the fire. "We do business. Our best valve is licensed from Tanaka Instruments."

"Sam Garnet went to Japan a lot?"

"We all make trips," Hook said. "Sergeant, I say look at Sam Garnet's women. That was his weak spot."

"Yeh," Wood said. "Thanks, Mr. Hook."

*

Alice Garnet worked on a painting. The steady rain depressed her with a sense of being alone. She worked silently, intensely, concentrating on the colors, the feel of the brushes.

The knock on her door was sharp, yet nervous. She looked at the door. The knocking came again, urgent. She went slowly to the door. George Thesiger stood in the gray rain.

"Can I talk to you?" he said.

He followed her into her apartment. She lit a cigarette.

"Sam never had a will, did he?" Thesiger asked.

"No. His lawyer called me."

"Then you get it? Money, stocks, holdings?"

"There wasn't much money. Sam knew he couldn't take it with him. Paper holdings."

"But forty percent of River Enterprises."

She smoked. "It seems so."

"What're you going to do about that stock?"

Alice picked up a paint brush, studied the canvas she had

been working on, smoked. "What have you got in mind, George?"

Thesiger sat down in the small, cluttered living room. He wiped his hands with his handkerchief, sweated in the raw day.

"Look, I don't have the cash to buy you out now, but I've got a few thousand for an option—and your proxy. Vinnie Tugela's getting the employees on my side. In a few years I'll buy your share, or go on running it for you, whichever you want."

Alice painted. "Can you run the business, George?"

"You think I can't? Sam tell you that? He had the silent votes, ran it his way. Well, he's dead, and I'll run River now."

She stopped painting. "You're glad Sam's dead."

"What?" Thesiger wiped his face. "I'm sorry, I didn't mean it that way. But he's gone, and—"

"You meant it, George."

"All right! He pushed me around for years, laughed at me. Now it's my turn. My chance, I'm not going to miss it."

She put out her cigarette. "Maybe you made your chance."

"Made? You think that I—?"

"You were the last to see Sam, except Vinnie Tugela. Why was he hiding in that motel? Some problem at River Enterprises?"

"I never touched Sam." Thesiger was up, his face glistening. "I don't know what he was doing."

"But he's dead, and you want my proxy for his forty percent," Alice Garnet said. "I'll think about it, George."

Thesiger watched her. "Has someone else talked to you? One of Sam's secret partners? I know some of them.

Tucker, Jim Pearson, maybe the Sheriff. They can't run the business, Alice." He seemed to think. "Maybe I should deal with them, leave you out."

"I said I'd think about it," Alice said.

George Thesiger wiped his hands. Then he walked out of the apartment. Nervous and hurrying.

*

Wood got to his desk just before lunch. Detective Phil Martin was waiting for him. Martin had his notebook out.

"Anne Thesiger says she was at an art gallery party in San Vicente the night Garnet got shot," Wood said. "Check on who saw her, and when. Try a Mrs. Glenda Forbes, and the gallery director, Peter Eyk."

Martin made a note. "I had a long talk with Berkeley," he said. "The Ikeda girl was a top student in Osaka. She asked for the exchange deal a year ago, turned down one chance because she only wanted UC-Berkeley. She's in one class with Alan Pearson—marine biology, which is funny because she's a history major. She's in the science club with Alan, too. She only dated one other guy—a friend of Alan's. She dated him before she met Alan, dropped him as soon as she did meet Alan. Her work's below par."

"Something on her mind?" Wood said.

"Yeh, so I cabled Japan. Seems she worked briefly for a company in her home town—Tanaka Instruments. They've got a close business connection to Hook Instruments, and I found something else. Twelve years ago, the girl's brother Yukio worked for Tanaka. He quit in 1962, no one's seen him since."

Wood forgot about lunch.

8

At the country club Alan Pearson and Jitsuko Ikeda had gone. Wood drove in the rain to the big Pearson house in Brandwater. The housekeeper opened the door, watched while Wood hung up his slicker, stamped his feet dry on a large mat inside the door.

James Pearson and his wife were eating lunch in a small family dining room. Celia Pearson looked at Wood as if sure she knew him from somewhere. Her thin hands went up to her hair, smoothing it. James Pearson stood up.

"I'm sorry, Sergeant. My wife isn't feeling—"

"I don't want your wife, Mr. Pearson. I want Alan and the Ikeda girl."

"They're at the country club, swimming. Now please—"

"No," Wood said. "I've been to the club. There's something wrong, Mr. Pearson. What do you know about the girl?"

"The girl?" Celia Pearson said. "A fine girl. Pretty. From Japan, you see? Small, the Japanese. Young."

"A very nice girl, Celia," Pearson said. He touched his wife's shoulder, turned to Wood. "What do you mean by something being wrong, Sergeant?"

"I've got a hunch Miss Ikeda isn't what she seems to be," Wood said. "Could Sam Garnet have been mixed up in anything in Japan? In any kind of trouble?"

"Trouble? No, I don't—"

The sound of the cup falling, breaking, was sharp in the small dining room. Celia Pearson's hand was rigid in the air above the table. The thin woman shook, her face white and haggard. Her throat convulsed as if she was fighting nausea.

"I . . . I . . ." She stood up, holding to her chair. Her face cleared, the color coming back. "Not what she seems, yes. You never do know, do you? You wait, and you look, and she is so pretty, and then . . . Trouble? Yes, terrible—"

Her face drained again, almost translucent, and she turned and vomited across the rug. James Pearson jumped to her side, held her. His voice soothed and called for the housekeeper at the same time. Celia Pearson clung to him. She was laughing and shivering. The housekeeper hurried in.

"Take her up," Pearson said. "It's all right, dear. Something you ate. Give her the sedative, Frieda. Just walk slowly, Celia. You'll be fine soon."

Still soothing, talking softly to her, Pearson walked his wife to the door out of the room. Wood turned to leave—and saw the white Porsche through the window. It was parked behind the big house. James Pearson spoke over his shoulder:

"Sergeant, some other time, please. Any time, but not—"

"I'm sorry, Mr. Pearson, I know Alan's here."

"My wife—!"

"I've got to talk to Alan and the girl," Wood said.

Pearson looked back at Wood, then looked at his wife. He nodded to the housekeeper.

"All right, yes. Take her upstairs, Frieda. I'll be up in a few minutes. Hurry."

Pearson watched his wife go.

"Where is Alan?" Wood said.

"In the cottage, I expect. I . . . I didn't want to walk in on him, you understand? He's not a child, but . . . Let's find them, then."

Wood followed the tall executive. Out of the house, they ran through the rain to the guest cottage. Pearson knocked on the sheltered door.

"Alan? Open the door, please. The police want to talk to you. Sergeant Wood."

There was a long silence. Then the door opened.

*

Alan Pearson stood angry at the foot of the double bed. Bare to the waist, his boyish chest pale and his belt loose, he glared at his father and Wood.

"We've got the vote now, you know, Dad."

Jitsuko Ikeda sat on the bed in a red kimono. Her dark eyes glinted with a sense of her power under the kimono. Watchful.

"I apologize, Alan," James Pearson said, his voice only a little stiff. "Sergeant Wood insisted on talking to you. I'll leave you with him; your mother—"

"You better stay, Mr. Pearson," Wood said, faced the Japanese girl. "Miss Ikeda, you arranged to meet Alan. Why? So he'd bring you down here? Is that what you were after?"

"You're crazy!" Alan exclaimed. "Suko just happened to—"

"Be in your marine biology class—when she's a history major?" Wood said. "Joined your science club, made friends with one other man who just happened to be a friend of yours? She just happened to pick UC-Berkeley, when she could have gone to another university six months earlier? Pure accident that she once had a job at Tanaka Instruments, a company tied to Hook Instrument?"

James Pearson said, "Sakai is a large suburb, Sergeant. I'm sure that Jitsuko had no idea Tanaka and Hook—"

"Miss Ikeda?" Wood said.

The tiny girl sat silent. Her eyes flat and opaque.

"Suko?" Alan said. "Tell him."

Jitsuko drew the kimono tighter around her. She turned her face to Alan, then turned away. Her soft voice was low:

"No, the policeman is right," she said. "I planned to meet Alan, to come here. I . . . I had good reason, but . . . Now I am not sure. Perhaps I was wrong."

"You knew Sam Garnet?" Wood asked. "Your brother did?"

"I did not know Mr. Garnet," Jitsuko said. "I came only to find what happened to my brother Yukio."

She brushed at her eyes, roughly. "My parents died when I was a baby, my grandparents died in the war. There was only Yukio, and my uncle who raised us. Twelve years ago Yukio was twenty, I was only seven. Yukio went away. He did not come back. Last year my uncle died, I was alone. It is sad to be alone."

Her eyes were dry, hard. "I found the letter in my uncle's documents. From America; from Monteverde, California; from Yukio." She got up, crossed the cottage bedroom to her suitcase. She took a single sheet of stationery from a zippered pocket. "The date is March 19, 1962. From The Rosa Hotel."

Wood took the letter. It was in Japanese, except for the printed letterhead. Cheap hotel stationery. James Pearson held out his hand.

"I read Japanese, Sergeant."

Wood gave him the letter. Pearson read it aloud:

"*Uncle, sir: All goes well. The man Garnet is a policeman here, he is to meet me this night. He will have much money, I will be rich, and soon will be home with you. The Americans can pay for all they have done. With honorable respect, Yukio.*"

Jitsuko sat on the bed again. "After I read that letter, I took a job at Tanaka. I found the name of Sam Garnet as a vice-president of Hook Instrument in America—in Monteverde, California! Hook Instrument has close dealings with Tanaka. My brother came to America and did not return. So I made inquiries, found that the Mr. Pearson who was president of Hook Instrument in Monteverde had a son at the university in Berkeley. I applied to come to Berkeley. I met Alan; he soon invited me to his home."

She smiled on the bed, a girl old for her years, aware of her power to make a man do what she wanted. She looked at Alan and stopped smiling.

"I am sorry, Alan."

"Revenge?" Alan said. "For your brother?"

The girl said nothing. Wood turned to James Pearson.

"Sam Garnet lived in Japan?" he asked.

"We were both there during the Korean War."

"Not since?"

"Some trips, yes. On business."

"This Yukio Ikeda was after money," Wood said, and

said to the girl, "What did your brother do in Japan, Miss Ikeda?"

"He was a clerk at Tanaka Instruments," Jitsuko said.

Wood thought. "Mr. Pearson, could Yukio Ikeda have learned something at Tanaka to blackmail Sam Garnet with?"

"I can't imagine what," Pearson said. "Sam said nothing."

"Dad?" Alan said. "Doesn't almost half your business come from that special electronic valve Tanaka developed?"

"We have the exclusive license, yes," Pearson agreed, "but there is nothing wrong in that arrangement. Nothing."

"And Sam Garnet wasn't working for Hook Instrument then, was he?" Wood said. "When did he join the company?"

"In May, I believe," Pearson said, his voice uneasy.

"May, 1962?"

"Yes," Pearson said.

"About the same time, *after* Yukio Ikeda wrote that letter," Wood said. "And Mr. Hook helped get Sam in the police, right?"

"Yes, Cornelius recommended Sam to the Chief back in 1952," Pearson said. "Sam was a policeman for ten years."

Wood nodded. "Miss Ikeda, this letter is all you ever heard from Yukio, or about him?"

"There was a statement from the shipping line when my uncle asked about Yukio," Jitsuko said. "Yukio had come to America as a sailor. The captain reported him as missing."

"To American authorities?"

"Yes. There was no result. Yukio was not found."

James Pearson said, "You mean he jumped ship? Then he was in the country illegally. He could simply be hiding still."

"Did you talk to Sam Garnet when you arrived, Miss Ikeda?" Wood asked. "Did he talk to you, maybe?"

"No," the girl said.

Alan said, "But he heard her *name* at the airport!"

"Yeh," Wood said. "Alan, that ring stone we found, it is yours, isn't it? You went to Sam Garnet's house that night."

"I told you I lost—" the boy insisted.

"No," Jitsuko said. "Alan gave his ring to me, Sergeant. I went to Mr. Garnet's house that night. We have lied to you."

Wood nodded, waited.

"Alan left me about one A.M. I watched him drive away, and saw a car parked. When Alan returned at two-thirty, the car was still there. Soon after, it, too, drove away. I—"

"What kind of car?" Wood said.

"Dark and old, a Buick," Jitsuko said. "I thought perhaps it had been Mr. Garnet. Watching me, yes? I was sure he knew of Yukio, so I walked to his house. It was dark. I thought I heard a sound at the side. The French doors were open, the office had been searched. But the house was empty. I left quickly, and must have knocked the stone from Alan's ring."

The others were all silent when she finished her story.

"That's all, Miss Ikeda?" Wood said.

She nodded.

"All right, but stay in town."

"I have acted badly. I will go to a motel."

"Don't be foolish," James Pearson said. "You'll stay here."

The girl smiled shyly. Grateful, or an act? Wood went out to his car. Alan Pearson said nothing.

*

Alan Pearson sat in a dark corner of the cottage. Jitsuko still sat on the bed. They were alone. Outside the rain poured down.

"You just wanted to use me, Suko?" Alan said.

"Yes," she said. "That was why I met you. But now—?"

"You told Sergeant Wood I was out when Sam Garnet died."

She looked away. "We have lied too much. You did not kill."

"Didn't I?" Alan said. "To find your brother, or what happened to him? That's why? Maybe revenge?"

"Yes, that was why," she said.

"Nothing more, Suko?"

"No." Her dark eyes reflected the gray light.

"All right," Alan said. "I'll help you. We'll try to find out what happened to Yukio. I was only seven then, but I seem to remember something, trouble. There was a woman, a girl I guess, my nursemaid. Sam Garnet's girl, I think."

Jitsuko sat on the bed, her eyes alert.

"My mother never had much time for me," Alan said. "Nursemaids, housekeepers, my Aunt Anne taking care of me. I suppose I never had real love, I suppose I want it. I have to believe you, don't I, Suko?"

The girl left the bed, went to him.

*

At headquarters, Wood went through the old files. If Yukio Ikeda had been reported for jumping ship, and was known to be somewhere in California twelve years ago, there should be a record. There was—a tracer sent out from San Pedro.

Wood read the tracer at his desk. He'd been a young rookie then. The name of the investigating detective wasn't Sam Garnet. Yukio Ikeda, seaman on the *Ise-Maru*, left his ship on March 15, 1962, was seen boarding a bus north. On March 20, Captain Kyosho Yamata reported Ikeda missing. The tracer went out from San Pedro, and an investigation was made in Monteverde.

A bus driver reported that a Japanese youth from San Pedro had left his bus in Monteverde on March 15. The youth was finally traced to The Rosa Hotel on March 24. A Yukio Ikeda had registered on March 15, checked out March 22. Further investigation turned up two witnesses who had seen a youth fitting Ikeda's description board the San Francisco bus March 22. The results were sent to San Francisco for further investigation, reported to San Pedro, and the case dropped.

There was no return report from San Francisco, and no more tracers from San Pedro. Wood picked up his telephone.

"Phil? Call San Pedro for the final disposition of an illegal entry trace on Yukio Ikeda, March 21, 1962. Call Frisco for the result of our report to them on Ikeda, March 26, 1962. And find out who owned, or managed, The Rosa Hotel here in 1962."

Wood hung up, waited, picked up the receiver again, and ordered some lunch sent in. Then he closed his eyes, sat back.

9

Wood had just finished lunch when Phil Martin reported.

"San Francisco never got a positive trace on Yukio Ikeda. It's a big town. They had a dozen bus drivers remembered Japanese or Chinese passengers, but nothing definite on Ikeda."

"All gooks look alike, yeh," Wood said. "San Pedro?"

"All tracers negative. Yukio Ikeda was never reported."

"The Rosa Hotel?"

"H-R Management, Incorporated, still owns it; manager there in 1962 died. You want me to talk to the owners about then?"

"I want," Wood said.

He hung up and saw the two men in front of his desk. Sheriff John Hoak, up from San Vicente, was a stocky man of fifty, with a bland face that revealed nothing. Lee Beckett, Chief Investigator for the County Prosecutor, was a big man who seemed as thick as he was wide, his blue eyes sunk in wind creases.

"Vause said you'd be in touch," Sheriff Hoag said.

"I thought it was a city case."

Hoag reddened. "Don't think, Sergeant. This case—"

"Get out of here, Sheriff!" Wood flung the remains of his lunch into his wastebasket. "I've been driving my ass off for two days, now I'm supposed to listen to politics? It's my case, I work on it, or get Vause to take me off!"

"He's got a murder," Lee Beckett said. "We've got politics. He's right, Hoag."

Sheriff Hoag walked to a window, looked out at the rain. The other detectives in the squad room bent to their work. Lee Beckett sat down, lit a cigarette.

"Hard day?"

"The rain, I guess," Wood said.

"Give Hoag a break. Old Cornelius Hook's been calling him and Tucker all day. About you badgering his sick daughter, his grandson, his busy son-in-law."

"Which son-in-law?"

"Both, I guess."

Sheriff Hoag left the window, walked to Captain Vause's office. He came out a second later. Vause wasn't in. Lee Beckett watched the Sheriff leave. Wood knew Beckett's record—a one-time New York police captain. A professional.

"You like to fill me in?" Beckett said. "Advisory?"

Wood filled him in on the case so far. Beckett thought.

"You think Sam Garnet was watching the girl?"

"No, he was at the motel. Someone else."

"Using Garnet's own gun sounds like an unplanned murder," Beckett said. "You think the murderer searched the house, too?"

"Maybe, maybe not. The Ikeda girl told me something extra, right? Alan Pearson was out running around that night."

"The Pearsons may have a rocky marriage. Rumors."

"Most of them from Anne Thesiger, I hear," Wood said. "She hated Garnet, but maybe not as much as it looked."

Beckett considered. "I heard that George Thesiger was Celia Hook's boy friend before she met Jim Pearson. Twenty-four years ago, but some people don't forget."

"The Ikeda girl was alone after one A.M.," Wood said. "What about Jim Pearson? He was in Japan in 1951, speaks Japanese."

"Quiet man, steady, but tense. Doesn't seem flashy, but he doubled Hook Instrument's business. Even old Hook admits that."

"Everyone says Garnet was a woman-chaser," Wood said. "Him and Jitsuko Ikeda? Alan jealous?"

"She's pretty young. Unless it was recent. Maybe she was down here in Monteverde before, looking for the brother."

Wood looked toward the windows and the rain. "Twelve years ago, Sam Garnet was a cop. Yukio Ikeda was off a ship from Japan. He expected money from Garnet—big money from the sound. It could be Yukio Ikeda was selling something, or delivering something."

"Maybe Japan can tell you? That ship captain, if he's still around. Or Ikeda might have had a record over there."

"I'll cable the Osaka police."

Beckett got up. "Call me if you want any help. I'll tell Tucker to keep Hoag quiet for you."

Beckett left the squad room, and Harry Wood went on looking out the windows at the rain. Steady rain in a semidesert is hard and depressing, like murder itself. Not the act, but the cold, gray chase. Pursued and pursuer like the water flowing off the hard desert clay, unable to sink down anywhere.

*

Alan and Jitsuko followed the Mexican houseman into Cornelius Hook's glass-walled study. The glass wall faced the surging Vaal Creek, dripped rain. Old Hook was reading.

"Come in, Alan." Hook closed his book. "Is this your lady?"

"Jitsuko Ikeda, Grandfather. Suko, my Grandfather, Cornelius Hook."

"I'm glad to meet you, young lady," the old man smiled.

Jitsuko bent her head, stood back.

"Grandfather," Alan said, "the police—"

"I know about the police, and about your ring. Your father called, naturally. Now tell me about the brother."

Alan told the old man about Jitsuko's scheme to find some trace of her missing brother. Hook got up, walked to his wall of glass. He had a ponderous, rolling walk on his short legs.

"Rain is good for my roses, but not for much else," he said. He turned. "You're sure Miss Ikeda didn't murder Sam Garnet? She tricked you into bringing her to Monteverde, meeting Garnet."

"She only wants to know about her brother!"

"Perhaps." Hook studied the girl. "You say your brother vanished here in Monteverde?"

"No," Jitsuko said. "Only that his last letter to my uncle came from here."

"With Sam Garnet's name in it, a meeting, and some plan?"

"That Yukio would soon have money."

"Garnet was a policeman then. Could he have met your brother in Japan?"

"I do not think so," Jitsuko said. "But it is possible."

Alan said, "Was Garnet in Japan between 1952 and 1962?"

"A good point. I don't really know," Hook said. "And you don't know why your brother was in Monteverde, Miss Ikeda?"

"No."

The old man watched the angry Vaal Creek below.

"Grandfather," Alan said. "Mother is sick again."

Hook stared out his windows.

"Very sick, I think. This morning," Alan said. "Was Sam Garnet more than a friend? Did Yukio Ikeda know that?"

"Don't be stupid, boy," Hook said. "Aunt Anne again, eh?"

"I know her better than I know Mother. Her, Frieda, all the nursemaids. Dad had to work too hard to be mother, too."

"Your Aunt Anne is a chronic malcontent, if she is my daughter. She needs a lesson." Hook turned now. "Twelve years ago I knew Sam Garnet as well as anyone. We were studying him then for our security-chief position. I don't recall a Japanese boy, or any trouble. Of course, he wouldn't have told us if there was."

"Maybe Yukio Ikeda knew something that would have cost him the security job," Alan said. "He would have—"

"He would have acted, yes," Hook said. "But, then, why is he murdered twelve years later? For what, Alan? Revenge?"

Jitsuko Ikeda met the old man's eyes.

"No," Alan said. "You remember Roberta Dunn, Grandfather? She took care of me as far back as I can remember, the only real mother I had then. She left when I was seven—twelve years ago. I cried for days, so I know when it was. Mother must have been away, because Dad took care of me for a while, and then Aunt Anne did until Mother came home."

"Yes, a pleasant girl."

"I remember Sam Garnet hanging around the house, laughing with her, kissing her when I was supposed to be asleep."

"She liked Sam, I believe. A vulnerable girl, though, and he wasn't the faithful type. I think that's why she left."

"She could have seen Yukio Ikeda, know something."

Hook nodded. "It's certainly worth a try. If you can find her now."

"I can find her," Alan said.

*

Harry Wood found George Thesiger behind the deserted parking lots of The River Inn, the roadhouse not yet open for the evening. Thesiger was watching the heaving Santa Rosa River.

"The Inn's on high enough ground," Wood said.

"I hope so," Thesiger said.

They went inside to Thesiger's office. The heavy man swept what looked like bank statements into his desk drawer.

"What can I do for you?" Thesiger asked. "I've got work."

"Busy?"

"I lost a partner."

"Partners a long time? Say, twelve years ago?"

Thesiger shook his head. "Not that long, more like eight, but I knew Sam twenty years." He scowled. "Why twelve years?"

"A Jap boy named Yukio Ikeda was here twelve years ago. He used Sam Garnet's name in a letter. No word of him since."

Thesiger whistled. "Like that? Who was this Ikeda?"

"A kid with ideas about making money."

"Don't we all? Ikeda? Any relation to Alan's new girl?"

"Older brother," Wood said. "You ever hear of him?"

"No." Thesiger frowned. "Sam was still a cop then?"

"Yeh. You know of trips he could have made to Japan?"

"Not until he joined Hook Instrument. He and Jim Pearson were over there in the Korean War. Celia, too, for a year or so. That's when they all got close. Jim came home into the company, Sam became a cop here, but they stayed close."

"The Pearsons and Garnet were together in Japan in 1951?"

"Sure were, on some small base."

"You knew Celia Hook before Pearson did, right?"

"Don't remind my wife of that," Thesiger said. "Kid stuff. I met Anne *before* Jim Pearson met Celia. It's still important to Anne that I picked her, didn't settle for her."

"Was there ever anything between Celia and Garnet?"

Thesiger shifted in his chair. "I don't know. Jim and Celia don't have what I'd call a marriage—separate bedrooms, separate vacations sometimes, Jim lives in his office —but it takes all kinds. Celia's delicate, maybe it's only that. Jim and Sam never stopped being friends."

"Celia Pearson was always delicate? Sickly?"

"Sort of delicate, maybe, but not sickly when I first knew her. High-strung, sensitive, but athletic, too. Fun, then."

"When did she change? Get sick?"

"I'm not sure. Before Alan was born."

"Did anything happen around March, 1962? Anything you might remember?"

"Christ, 1962? No way, Sergeant. Do you remember 1962?"

"Some things," Wood said. "For instance, Sam Garnet was hired by Hook Instrument in 1962. In May. Remember that?"

"Yeh, I do," Thesiger nodded. "We had a dinner for Garnet, all of us . . . Hold it. No, not Celia. She was away, had to be, because Alan was staying with Anne and me. I don't—"

Thesiger snapped his fingers. "Sure, the nurse quit! Now I see it. Celia went to visit friends in Palm Springs around March that year, Anne and I drove her down, stayed a few weeks ourselves. When we got back, Jim Pearson was going nuts. Alan's nurse had quit, she'd been with the kid almost since he was born, so he took it hard. Jim had to take care of Alan until we got back, and Anne took over until Celia came home and hired a girl."

"The nurse quit suddenly? After seven years?"

"Yeh. A nice girl, heavy, sweet on Sam Garnet, too. Sure, I remember that now. Alan threw a real fit over the nurse and Garnet. Maybe that's what started Alan not liking Sam."

"What was the nurse's name?"

"Dunn. Roberta Dunn. She's still around somewhere."

*

It was dark when Anne Thesiger opened her door to her father. Cornelius Hook pushed past her into the pastel-blue living room. He took out a cigar, lit it without taking his eyes off Anne.

"What do you know about Sam Garnet's murder?"

"Only that I like it," Anne said.

"That's the first thing you'll stop, remarks like that."

"I don't know anything, of course."

"That's the second thing," Hook said. "From now on that's all you or George know—nothing. The third thing is no more about Celia and Garnet. Not to the police or to Alan."

Anne protested. "I never—"

"You've been doing it since before Alan was born, but no more. What do you know about Alan's Jap girl?"

"I think she's pretty clever."

"So do I. Twelve years ago her brother came to Monteverde. Yukio Ikeda. You ever hear of him, remember anything?"

"No."

"All right. From now on this family says nothing. Clear?"

"Don't browbeat me!" Anne said. She sat down. "Will you offer George the vice-presidency, help me make him take it?"

"Does he have to be made to take it?"

"I'm not sure. He has some plans, I think. Something on his mind. He hasn't told me what, but he's taken five thousand dollars from our bank. About all the cash he has."

"You don't know what for?"

"No."

Old Hook chewed on his cigar. "I'll talk to him."

"I want him in the company, Father."

"You always have," Hook said. He smoked. "Celia's sick. Jim thinks it's bad this time, a real relapse."

"I'm sorry, it's been quite a while. How is Alan taking it?"

Hook shrugged. "He's grown now, busy with the Jap girl. He's trying to help her locate something about her brother. He thinks that old nurse of his, Roberta Dunn, can help. Maybe she can. You're sure you know nothing about this Yukio Ikeda?"

"No more than I know what happened to Celia twenty-two years ago, Father."

Cornelius Hook walked out of the house.

10

Harry Wood sloshed through the flowing puddles to Alice Garnet's apartment door. She wore a dark green robe, her copper hair loose on her shoulders. Her eyes were tired.

"You look drowned," she said.

"I feel drowned," Wood said. "A salmon swimming upstream."

"I'll get some coffee."

Wood sat in the cluttered little living room. He looked around at the disorder of living and painting as if he liked it. Parkinson's Law—when everything is orderly it's dead, no longer alive and growing. Alice Garnet's room was very alive. She brought his cup of coffee, sat and sipped one herself.

"News, Sergeant?" she asked.

"Some," he said. "You like living alone, Alice? Not like Sam? No men?"

Her smile was self-mocking. "No men, Harry."

"A woman like you? There's got to be a reason. Bad affair?"

She drank coffee. "Not exactly bad. I'm one of those women who met one man once and never got over it. The doormat. Funny, isn't it? I was seventeen, it lasted a long time, no ring."

"Why not?"

"It just wasn't in the cards."

"Who was he?"

"A man. Donny. A boy, all right? What news is there?"

The rumble of the Santa Rosa River filled the room. Wood told her about Yukio Ikeda, the letter twelve years ago.

"That Japanese girl met Alan on purpose? To get down here and close to Sam?" Alice said. "You think he knew her?"

"He knew the name, maybe," Wood said. "He was a cop then. Do you remember him going to Japan much?"

"No, not after Korea. Until he joined Hook Instrument."

"Did Sam have money back then? Own his boat?"

"Not that I remember. The security position at Hook was a big financial step up. He was pleased as punch, greedy."

"There was a woman back then, Roberta Dunn. Sam was giving her a hard time, maybe. Alan Pearson's nursemaid."

"Yes, a vulnerable girl. Worse than me." She smiled, mocking again. "Sam hurt her a lot. She had to go away."

"You know her?"

"Very well. She lives in Fremont now, a schoolteacher. We still talk sometimes. About Sam. She still beats herself."

Wood looked at his watch. It was five-thirty.

"How about some dinner?"

"All right. I'll just change."

Wood lit a cigarette, smoked as he listened to her dressing in her bedroom.

*

The white Porsche parked in front of a small, stucco house in one of the cheaper sections of Fremont. Gas flames burned in the night at the refineries to the north through the rain. Alan Pearson and Jitsuko rang the bell. A woman opened the door.

"Alan! How nice. Isn't this rain awful? Come in."

She herded them inside. In her early forties, she had heavy hips and thighs, and her hands plucked at her graying hair. A round, girlish face.

"Well, introduce me to your friend, Alan."

"Jitsuko Ikeda, Miss Dunn," Alan said. "Miss Dunn, we're looking for Suko's brother. Yukio Ikeda. He was in Monteverde twelve years ago. He disappeared. We think his disappearance could have some connection to Sam Garnet's murder."

Roberta Dunn gripped the back of a chair. She touched her heavy breast with one hand.

"I . . . I read it in the paper. Who—?" She shook her head, held onto the chair. "Poor Sam, he didn't treat me very well, but that was his way. He made no promises. It seems ludicrous now, doesn't it? An overweight schoolteacher and Sam Garnet? I was thirty then, taking care of another woman's child. Sam was . . . Well, no matter. I had some moments." She seemed to see those moments twelve years ago. "Do they know who . . . did it, Alan?"

"I don't think so," Alan Pearson said. "Miss Dunn, do you remember anything about a Japanese man back then? A kid, really, twenty. He jumped his ship, wrote a letter from Monteverde that mentioned Sam Garnet and some kind of money plan."

"Twelve years?" Roberta Dunn shook her head. "I was busy with you, and with . . . Sam. I had hopes, you see?"

She let her voice fade. "Well, a Japanese boy? I don't think so."

"In March, Miss Dunn. He wrote a letter home on March 19, 1962. He was going to meet Sam Garnet."

"I see." Roberta Dunn nodded. "March? Well, I think it must have been about March that year when your mother went on vacation. Your father was so busy, as usual, and Mrs. Thesiger and her husband drove your mother. I was alone taking care of you, I remember that. It gave me time to meet with Sam Garnet, you see? Every chance I got. You didn't like it, I'm afraid. I suppose it was wrong, with a child so near, but—"

She hesitated. "I *do* seem to remember a time. Yes, Sam was in your house with me, and he left to talk to someone outside. A small man, perhaps Japanese, but it was dark. You began to cry, so I was busy quieting you. Sam came back in, and we . . . But he had to leave very soon after. There was a car outside waiting for Sam, someone else driving."

Jitsuko said, "Did you see this man outside, hear him?"

"Not really, dear, just a glimpse. Sam never talked about his work," Roberta Dunn said. "But . . . perhaps—?"

"Perhaps what, Miss Dunn?" Alan said.

"Well, I might have seen a Japanese boy around your house a few days earlier. Before your mother went on vacation. Only your father had Japanese gardeners then. They had friends."

"If you do think of something, call me, okay?" Alan said.

"Yes, of course," she said. "Poor Sam, he was so . . ."

She didn't finish what Sam Garnet had been, and Alan and Jitsuko left.

When they had gone, Roberta Dunn smoothed the chairs

in her living room, then made her dinner. Her eyes seemed to look into space as she cooked. Abstracted, she ate her dinner in front of her television set. She stared at the rectangle of dancing blue-white light, and suddenly stopped eating. She seemed to think, looked at her telephone, began to eat faster. She had just finished her dinner, the seven-thirty show was starting on the TV, when a car stopped outside.

Roberta Dunn got up quickly, hurried to her front door. "Alan? I'm so glad you came back. I *do* remember—!" She peered into the rain. "Alan? Is that—?"

*

Wood and Alice Garnet ate dinner at a steak house near the freeway. They talked about Sam Garnet, what might be hidden somewhere in his past. Wood paid the check, waited while Alice fixed her face. When she was ready, he took her arm.

"Let's go and see this Roberta Dunn."

In his car, Wood could feel Alice Garnet close beside him. The freeway to Fremont flowed with a film of water. All the creeks were high under the bridges.

"Why didn't you ever marry?" Alice asked.

"Took care of my father until a few years ago. He was sick. My job keeps me busy. Most women don't want a cop's life."

"Policemen do marry."

"Pinch and scrape. I guess I like women who don't want to pinch and scrape. Special women."

"No woman is special, Harry. You can play us like fish if you know how and try hard enough."

"I guess I never wanted a woman I had to play like a fish. One-to-one, she wants me as much as I want her."

The gas flames of the refineries flickered high in the night as they reached Fremont. Its streets were deserted in the rain. Wood slowed as they entered an area of small houses.

"Perdido Street," Alice said. "Three blocks."

Wood located the small stucco house. He got out of the car and turned back quickly. Alice was getting out.

"Stay in the car!"

Wood went up the walk to the front door. The door was open. Lights were on inside, and a television set blared. Rain blew in through the open door, but the door itself wasn't blowing—something held the door, blocked the entrance. Wood bent down.

Alice Garnet hadn't stayed in the car. Behind Wood now, she made a low, sick sound.

Wood knelt over the body of a woman. A heavy woman. Shot once in the head, twice in the chest. A pool of blood was still liquid and spreading. Wood's watch read 7:50.

"Dead," he said. "Maybe twenty minutes. Is it—?"

"Roberta Dunn, yes," Alice said. "Harry?"

Her voice shook. Wood moved to her. She leaned against him, her face on his chest. Wood held her tight. She turned her face up, and Wood kissed her. Her breasts pressed against him, her belly moved warm.

Wood stepped away. "Take my car and go home."

"Harry—?"

"Go on now. I'll get a ride from the Fremont cops."

He gave her his car keys. She walked away. When his car was gone, Wood went into Roberta Dunn's house and called the Fremont police. He called Lee Beckett at the County Prosecutor's office, too.

*

Detective-Lieutenant Carra of the Freemont police watched the Coroner's men take out Roberta Dunn's body. The Prosecutor's investigator, Lee Beckett, watched Carra.

"She must have opened the door, got hit on the spot," Carra said. "No sign of anyone inside, no wet marks."

"Unless the killer was here long enough for marks to dry," Wood said.

Lee Beckett said, "The same case, Wood?"

"Roberta Dunn was Sam Garnet's girl friend twelve years ago," Wood said. "Alan Pearson's nurse, too. What was the gun, Carra?"

"A funny one. Eight-millimeter, hard lead bullets," Carra said. "Eight-millimeter, not nine."

Lee Beckett clicked his teeth. "Sounds like the 1914 Japanese army Nambu pistol. Not many eight-millimeter guns around."

"When?" Wood said.

"Doc says between seven and eight tonight," Carra said. "She was a schoolteacher, lived alone. Knew a lot of people, though. We'll start checking her out."

There was nothing more for Wood to do. No clues had been found in Roberta Dunn's house. A Fremont patrolman drove Wood to Monteverde headquarters. Wood's own car was there, a note on the front seat: *Call me tomorrow, please.*

There were no messages for Wood at his desk. He filled out his report and went home.

He lay in bed listening to the ceaseless rush of his creek. It wasn't the creek that made him lie awake. *Call me tomorrow.*

11

In the morning the county went on disaster alert. Some creeks were already over their banks, others threatened everywhere. They were piling sandbags along the Santa Rosa River as Wood drove to headquarters. He couldn't remember when he'd seen sandbags along the Santa Rosa.

Phil Martin was waiting for Wood. "I checked out on the owners of The Rosa Hotel. No one around then remembers Yukio Ikeda, but I got one interesting thing."

"What?"

"The night clerk back then was Vinnie Tugela. He went to work for Sam Garnet about six months later."

Wood listened to the rain. "Find out what kind of car Tugela drives. See if he knew a Roberta Dunn."

"The woman killed over in Fremont last night?"

"Yeh," Wood said. "Any answer to our cable to Osaka?"

"Not yet. Taking their time," Phil Martin said. "But we checked out Anne Thesiger's alibi for the night Garnet got his. She was at that gallery party, all right. Down in San Vicente. That Mrs. Forbes and the gallery director,

Peter Eyk, remembered her. Trouble is, they don't remember her much after one A.M."

Wood nodded moodily.

*

The Cuyama Beach marina was lashed with spray. Cornelius Hook walked slowly from his Cadillac to the *Sea King II* as if he hadn't noticed the rain and wind. Vinnie Tugela, in a dripping sou'wester, coiled rope on the foredeck.

"Come aboard, Mr. Hook," the big boatman said.

"I don't like boats," Hook said. "You called me?"

Tugela squatted easily on the rolling deck, wiped rain and spray from his mustache. "You lost a vice-president, Mr. Hook, and I lost a boss. We've got something going the same."

"Do we?"

"Yeh. I figure you lost more than a vice-president. A kind of partner too, right? I mean, you got a stake in River Enterprises, right? You, Jim Pearson, some other friends?"

"I have a lot of interests."

"I figure it's worth something to protect your interests."

"I always protect my interests," Hook said. "Do you want to spell it out for me before I drown?"

"I lost a good boss, Mr. Hook, one I could work with. A friend, you know? I knew where I stood, where we was going. He was going to let me operate the casino, maybe the Inn."

"You're worried about Alice Garnet?"

"In a way," Tugela said, balanced on the heaving deck. "Mr. Hook, someone's working fast to take Sam Garnet's place, be the boss at River Enterprises, run the whole operation."

"Run it? Who?"

"George Thesiger."

"George! He'd drive River Enterprises into the ground! He isn't capable of running something like River on his own."

"That's what I think," Tugela agreed. "I got a stake in River, you know? But he's already got me lining up the small fry for him, and he's after Garnet's forty percent from Alice."

"He doesn't have the money."

"Enough for an option, and her proxy to vote the shares."

"Have you agreed to help?"

"If he gets Alice Garnet's proxy, he's the boss. I got to protect myself. He's offered me cash, the boat, managing the Inn, and more. But—"

"But there'll be nothing to manage if he runs it."

"You've got a stake, too, right? You and your friends? He's not Sam Garnet, he won't listen to you, will he?"

"No," Hook said. "Not George."

Tugela stood up on the deck. "He wants it awful bad, his big chance to be important. Maybe he even made his chance, you know? Sam Garnet came back to Monteverde under cover, but someone found him, surprised him with his own gun. When Thesiger was here on the boat with me a couple of days ago, that Sergeant Wood came around. Thesiger didn't want to be seen with me."

"In the cabin," Hook said. "We'll talk."

Tugela held the boat for Cornelius Hook to climb aboard.

*

At Alice Garnet's apartment, the noise of the river was louder. Harry Wood barely heard it, becoming used to the sound already. Alice's copper hair was pulled back, severe, when she opened the door, and Roberta Dunn's dead body was still in her eyes.

"Have you found—?"

"No," Wood said.

The small apartment had been cleaned and straightened, as if Alice had needed to be busy. Wood closed the door. Alice kissed him, went to the couch and sat down. He sat beside her.

"You've lived in Monteverde all your life, Alice?"

"I was going to leave when I got out of high school. New York, study painting. Instead, I met Donny. I never went to New York or anywhere else. An artist can't make a living in Monteverde, so I went to work for the agency."

"Because you had this Donny?"

"Yes." She touched Wood's ear. "I was happy. He was a nice man, Harry, and he wanted me. That's important. He wanted me, yet he was always trying to let me go, be free of him."

"It sounds like he knew what he was doing," Wood said. "How long did it go on?"

"Too long. You think he calculated it all? An act? Perhaps he did; it didn't matter."

"But you didn't marry him."

"No."

She took her hand away from Wood's face, stared at space. Wood watched her. He changed the subject.

"When Sam was a cop, did he talk about Vinnie Tugela?"

"Yes. Sam's faithful retainer since Tugela was just a boy."

"Tugela'd do anything for Sam?"

"I think he would have."

"Sure? No chance of a double-cross? Tugela work against Sam for someone else? For enough money?"

"I doubt it, Harry. Only with a hobo like Tugela, who can be sure?"

"How did Sam meet Tugela? When?"

"It was while Sam was still a policeman. I don't know how," she said, turned. "You think Tugela could have murdered Sam?"

"Someone Sam trusted all the way. It has to be. Sam was a trained cop, and no fool. It had to be a complete surprise. Sam was relaxed, unsuspecting, his gun right out in sight."

"A friend," Alice said. She was silent. "I wonder if it matters who killed Sam? Will it help to punish? Perhaps Sam left no other way, no choice."

"Maybe not."

"Perhaps all murder victims really murder themselves, leave someone no other way out. Somewhere, the murderer is suffering now because of what Sam made him do. Perhaps the murderer is a better man than Sam was."

"That could be. But there's always another way."

"You're so sure, Harry?" She touched his face again. "Life is mostly what happens to you. What's done to you. Chance. We love who will love us, do what we find to do. After that it's only the small pleasures, the days and nights."

"You should have gotten out of this town."

"I may yet," she said, smiled. She stood up. "How about a drink? Some coffee?"

"No. Another ten minutes and I'd never leave."

"Good," Alice said.

He reached up to her. She bent, and they kissed. Then Wood got up, too.

*

In his office, James Pearson was dictating a letter when Cornelius Hook came in. The old man waited in front of the windows overlooking the cresting Santa Rosa River. Pearson nodded his secretary out, sat back and rubbed at his eyes.

"Have you thought about Thesiger?" Hook said from the windows. "Just the personnel department. A cozy shelf."

"I said it was all right," Pearson said. "It doesn't matter."

"It does to me." Hook came from the windows. "You know George has an idea of running River Enterprises? I wonder how long he's thought about it, or planned it."

"Planned?" Person laughed. "You think George could have murdered Sam Garnet?"

"You don't think that's possible?"

Pearson laughed harder. "I suppose anything is possible, Cornelius. Just about anything."

"I want George out of the way. Some of River's dealings are pretty thin-edged. Thesiger would have us all in jail."

James Pearson closed his eyes. "I had to send Celia down to the sanitarium. This morning."

Hook sat down. "All right, perhaps just as well. With the police all around, the river up. If the river goes over, you'll have a battle to save the plant."

"I have the buildings sandbagged, vital materiel up as high as we can get it. We should weather it," Pearson said. His eyes remained closed. "There's been another murder."

"Another? Who?"

"Roberta Dunn, Alan's old nurse. In Fremont."

"Sam Garnet's woman once, too," Hook said.

Pearson opened his eyes. "Who would kill such a woman?"

"You don't think it was the same murderer?"

Pearson sighed. "Yes, I suppose it was."

"Roberta Dunn," Hook mused. "She left you twelve years ago, about when that Yukio Ikeda was supposed to be here meeting Sam Garnet. Why did she quit back then, Jim? Did she ever say?"

"Who knows why servants leave? A better job."

"Did she stay Garnet's woman after she left?"

"I don't know, Cornelius. I doubt it."

"Her murderer is unknown, too?"

"As far as I know."

Hook took out a cigar, looked at it, put it away again. He got up, began to pace.

"Alan and that Ikeda girl were talking about Roberta Dunn at my house just last evening," Hook said. "They wondered if she could know anything about Yukio Ikeda. They said they were going to talk to the woman."

"Alan?" Pearson said.

"And the Jap girl. We better find out if they did go to Roberta Dunn. Alan, anyway."

"Yes," James Pearson said. He stood up.

"And don't forget about George Thesiger. Have the offer ready. Vice-president of Personnel."

James Pearson bent over his intercom, told his secretary to have his car brought to the front.

*

Wood fought the driving rain up the grade of Mesa Grande Pass. He found Hutter Road, turned off on the muddy blacktop road, drove on slowly. If his information from Lee Beckett was right, River Enterprise's floating gambling casino was in an isolated house up Hutter Road.

A half mile in from the Pass highway, Wood saw the white building ahead. Just a big farmhouse, but Wood's practiced eye could see where a lot of cars had parked all around it. Before he reached the house, a deep mountain creek ran under a wooden bridge. Debris had blocked under the bridge, the creek cascaded up over it, and the supports leaned and shook. Wood got out.

The blacktopping where the road met the bridge had already washed away leaving a widening gap. The heavy beam supports were trembling with the force of the blocked water. It was hard to tell how long the supports would hold. They might never give way, or they might go any second. One large boulder carried down the creek would collapse the bridge like a stack of twigs.

Wood looked across the bridge to estimate his chances. Vinnie Tugela stood on the far side in a short, yellow, sou'wester slicker.

"I wouldn't chance it," Tugela said.

12

Tugela had to shout across the distance, above the roar of the violent creek.

"Just made it across myself!"

The bridge shook and vibrated, the creek pouring across it between where Wood stood and Tugela on the far side.

"I can make it across walking!" Wood shouted.

"I don't know, Sergeant!" Tugela put his foot on a bridge support on the other side, pushed at the support. The big man grinned. "She could go any minute!"

The whole weakened bridge creaked under the small pressure of Tugela's foot. Balanced on a hair. Tugela kept his foot against the support, shook his head.

"Hate to see her go with you aboard, Sergeant. Not much chance in that creek."

The rain dripped down Wood's face as he looked at the big man across the white creek. He raised his voice higher above the roar.

"Twelve years ago, Tugela, a man named Yukio Ikeda checked into The Rosa Hotel. He wrote a letter home, used Sam Garnet's name, talked about making money. You were night clerk at The Rosa then. You remember Yukio Ikeda?"

"Twelve years?"

"How many Japanese checked into the hotel in those days?"

Tugela's answer blew away on a sudden, swirling gust of rain wind. Wood waited. Tugela looked upstream, shouted:

"What's The Rosa register say?"

"That Ikeda checked out on March 22, 1962!"

"So what do you want from me!"

"Ikeda's never been heard from since!"

"It's a big country!"

Across the rushing creek, near the white house beyond Tugela, a man came out into the rain. Even at that distance, Wood recognized George Thesiger. Wood looked at the shaking bridge again, tested it with a step. Vinnie Tugela glanced behind him, saw Thesiger at the house. Tugela turned back toward Wood across the bridge, leaned his weight on the support again. The whole structure leaned, teetered. Wood jumped back.

"It just ain't safe, Sergeant!" Tugela called. "You better go on back, you know? I've got business anyway."

Wood shouted, "Tracers were sent out on Ikeda in every city from L.A. to San Francisco. We turned him up in Monteverde, but it seems he left for San Francisco before we got to him. Only no trace of him since. Funny."

"He checked in, he checked out," Tugela called across. "If that's what the register says, okay? I guess he paid his bill, why would I remember him?"

"You remember Roberta Dunn?"

On the far side of the bridge, Tugela nodded. "Sam Garnet's woman once! Why?"

"She was murdered last night! Just like Sam!"

Across the creek, Vinnie Tugela took his foot off the bridge support. He wiped at his face, his mustache, seemed to look all around him. Near the white house, George Thesiger was gone.

Tugela shouted, "You know who did it, Wood?"

"Not yet! Do you?"

"No guess!"

"Roberta Dunn was around Sam Garnet back twelve years ago, too! Alan Pearson's nurse!"

"Garnet knew all kinds of people twelve years ago!"

"Bad people, Tugela? Did he have some business going?"

"Good and bad, Sergeant!" Tugela called across. "I got business to do. I don't know nothing about twelve years ago!"

The big man turned away from the bridge and the creek, his long hair matted by the rain. Wood called:

"What kind of car do you drive, Tugela?"

Tugela stopped, looked back over the creek. "A '72 Impala, red, okay?"

Wood watched the muscular roustabout until Tugela reached the distant white house. George Thesiger was nowhere in sight.

*

Jitsuko Ikeda looked at her face in the mirror of the Pearsons' cottage bedroom. Naked, she ran her hands down her smooth, full body. She smiled at her body, her own face.

A door slammed up at the big house. Jitsuko listened, then went to the cottage window. Alan Pearson was walking toward the cottage under an umbrella. Jitsuko watched the youth for a moment, then picked up her red kimono and went back to the mirror. She studied herself again, solemn now, and put on the kimono. She left it loose, her breasts just showing in soft curves, and went to open the door.

"Did you sleep okay?" Alan said.

"A little," Jitsuko said, kissed him.

"We'll find him, Suko—or what happened to him."

Jitsuko went to sit on the bed, her tiny feet curled up under her, the kimono slipping lower on her breasts. She pulled the robe closed, shook her head.

"Twelve years is very long. I have been foolish to try."

"Maybe not," Alan said. He perched on the arm of a couch. "I think your brother met Sam Garnet at this house back then. I think Miss Dunn saw him. Maybe Yukio was part of what's wrong in my family."

"There was a big car, early this morning," Jitsuko said. "Your mother got into it. She has gone somewhere?"

"To a sanitarium down in L.A. Dr. Fynn sent her."

"I am very sorry."

"She didn't even know me this morning," Alan said.

"Perhaps we should visit the sanitarium? Later."

"Dr. Fynn says no." Alan hunched forward. "Suko, you're sure you don't know what Yukio was doing in Monteverde?"

"No. I was seven then, Alan."

"Yeh," he said. "Could Yukio have been trying to blackmail Sam Garnet? Or someone?"

"Perhaps."

Alan looked up. "That doesn't bother you?"

"Bother?" Her dark eyes jumped. "Yes, of course, it would have been a bad thing. But how would Yukio do it, what could he have known? A boy from far away in Japan?"

Alan watched her, seemed to study her face. Uneasy, as

if puzzled by something he thought but didn't want to think.

"I think it must have been more that Yukio did some task for Mr. Garnet," Jitsuko said. "Some business matter."

"And vanished," Alan said. "Some—"

They both heard the steps this time. Splashing through the puddles on the lawn to the cottage. A light knock on the door. Alan went and opened the door. James Pearson came in. His handsome face was taut, drawn.

"Alan," Pearson said, "did you and Jitsuko visit Roberta Dunn last evening?"

"Yes, in Fremont."

"Together?" Pearson said. "When?"

"Both of us, yes. About five-thirty."

"What happened when you talked to her?"

"We asked about Yukio Ikeda. She remembered that maybe a Japanese man had come here to our house to see Sam Garnet."

Pearson brushed away what Roberta Dunn remembered. "Where did you go when you left Miss Dunn?"

"We came home. Suko had a headache, she wanted to rest here. You were out, Mother was in her room, so I went out to get some dinner."

"Straight home from Fremont? In the Porsche? Then you went out alone, left Jitsuko alone? Who saw you?"

"No one I knew. I just ate at a roadhouse."

Pearson bit his lip. "A fifteen-minute drive from Fremont in the Porsche," he calculated. "Fifteen minutes back. Make it forty-five minutes, longer for Jitsuko unless she had a car ready. Say an hour, or even an hour-and-a-half. What time did you leave Roberta Dunn?"

"About six o'clock. Dad—?"

"Roberta Dunn was murdered last night," Pearson said. "In her house. Shot. Between seven and eight o'clock."

"Shot?" Alan said. "And the police think that I—"

Pearson sat down, squeezed his face with his hands. "They will, Alan. They'll check. You or Jitsuko."

Jitsuko said, "And you, Mr. Pearson? You were also out. Your wife was alone. She was ill this morning."

"What?" James Pearson blinked at the girl. "Yes, that's so. They'll have to check us, I expect."

The cottage was cold and damp in the silent rain.

*

The flood emergency chaos brought a rash of burglaries to Monteverde, and Wood was busy until after lunch. When he got back to his desk, there was a note to call Lieutenant Carra.

"No motive yet," Carra said from Fremont, "but we got a lead. The Dunn woman had at least one visitor about six last night. Neighbor saw a white Porsche parked in front."

"The neighbor's sure it was a Porsche?"

"Absolutely. He's a car salesman."

"He hear any shots?"

"Too much wind and rain. Watching TV from seven on."

Wood hung up. A white Porsche was a hell of a car to go murdering in, and at six not seven-thirty. Still, killers can return. The duty-sergeant stood over Wood's desk.

"Visitor, Sergeant. A Jap. Send him in?"

"Send him in," Wood said.

The Japanese who came to Wood's desk was a small, neat man in a dapper gray suit. He sat down.

"Lieutenant Shimada, from Osaka," the Japanese man said. His voice was crisp in clear English. "I was in Los

Angeles. Your cable inquired about an exchange student, an illegal entry, so we thought I should report in person."

"Thanks, Lieutenant. What do you have?"

"First, there is no criminal record for Yukio Ikeda of Sakai. He was a clerk for Tanaka Instruments, sailed as a seaman on the *Ise-Maru* in January, 1962, aged twenty. Not heard of in Japan since. His uncle reported his disappearance in 1963, but our inquiries in Japan and in America were all negative."

"Could your people find the ship's captain?"

"Without trouble. He lives in Osaka, is retired. He recalls Yukio Ikeda well, the only man who jumped ship successfully under his command. He is positive that Ikeda took nothing ashore, had no package aboard or any other object."

"How can he be so sure?"

"Captain Yamata was a most careful man about what his crew brought on board and took ashore. Especially a new man. The day was warm. Later, other crewmen stated that Ikeda wore no coat, carried nothing. His personal effects were left behind."

"He had pockets, or under his clothes."

"True, but even heroin takes up some space for a shipment of any value. Without a coat, anything he carried would have been very small. It is, of course, possible. Jewels, for example, but Captain Yamata examined what his men brought *on* board, too, and Ikeda acted in no way suspicious."

"Did he talk to his bunkmates?"

"When my department explained to Captain Yamata that it was an American police matter, the Captain thought strongly. He at last recalled a crewman saying that Ikeda was given to staring out to sea when on watch, yet he was not a moody boy."

"Nothing special about his life in Japan?"

"Nothing. He had never been away from Sakai."

"Well, thanks, Lieutenant. If we can do any—"

"There is one more thing, Sergeant," Shimada said. "When my people checked at Tanaka, they found that two days before, someone had called Tanaka's personnel department to ask if a Jitsuko Ikeda was related to the Yukio Ikeda who had once worked for them. If she was, where could Miss Ikeda be reached? When told that Jitsuko was Yukio's sister, and was now in America, the caller thanked them and hung up immediately."

"That would have been three days ago now?"

"Yes. The caller gave no name. It was a local call. No way we can learn who it was or why he called."

"I think I can guess why," Wood said. "You're sure we can't do anything for you? Stay awhile?"

"It tempts me, Sergeant, but I must return to Los Angeles. If you need me, I will be there two weeks. The Biltmore Hotel."

Shimada left, and Wood picked up his phone.

"Phil? Tugela says he drives a red Impala, 1972. Does he?"

"That's his car."

"No Buick? Old, a dark color?"

"Now how'd you know that?" Phil Martin said. "There is a dark blue Buick, 1965. It's registered to River Enterprises."

"Thanks, Phil," Wood said.

13

Wood drove up the eroded barranca on the southwest outskirts of Monteverde. All at once the rain had stopped, a bright break in the sky to the north for the first time in almost three days. The green sportscar was still parked at the side of Vinnie Tugela's old farmhouse.

Wood didn't go into the house. He walked around the side to the rear. A dilapidated gray barn leaned against the sodden and muddy side of the steep barranca. Tire tracks led to it, and the door was locked. In the brightening afternoon, Wood peered in through a dirty and broken barn window. He saw the car—an old, dark blue Buick.

"What are you doing?"

The voice was behind him. A woman's voice, and scared. Wood turned and saw the tall blonde with the full breasts and hips. Virginia Gallo. She wore an old shirt and jeans now, and her long blonde hair was uncombed.

"Oh!" Relief all over her. "You're that cop."

"You're afraid of someone, Miss Gallo?"

"Out here a cat scares me, any noise." She shivered. "One more night here, I go ape."

"Then why stay?"

She grinned, shrugged.

"Where is Tugela?" Wood asked.

"On business. A real busy boy, Vinnie. Going places."

"Busy doing what?"

"I don't know."

"How many nights have you been out here, Miss Gallo?"

She laughed. "That'd be telling."

"Tell me anyway," Wood said. "Here or at headquarters."

"Hey! I mean—" her face closed up. "Look, I told you I don't know anything about Sam Garnet."

"How many nights, Miss Gallo?"

Her voice was sullen. "Three."

"So you were here the night Sam Garnet was shot?"

She nodded.

"Garnet was out of town, so Tugela moved in?"

"Sam Garnet didn't have a lock on me!"

"Where was Tugela that night?"

She tossed her hair. "Where do you think? With me."

"No," Wood said. "I already know he wasn't here, and this isn't some game. You want to be caught lying in a murder? Or weren't you here all that night yourself?"

"Me? I never—!" She stopped. "Playing us off? Well, I was out here all that night. I guarantee it."

"Alone? We'll get it out of Tugela anyway."

"Then why ask me?"

"Easier," Wood said. "Save myself work and time."

"Vinnie'd kill me."

"No he won't."

She resisted. "Vinnie didn't murder anyone. Too smart."

"I never said he did, but he knows more than he's told. I'm chasing a killer. I can't let people decide what to tell me, and what not to. They don't know what's important, and neither do I. Now, was Tugela here that night?"

She watched the muddy ground. "Not after nine o'clock."

"He was away in that old Buick back there?"

"Yes."

"When did he get back?"

"I guess it was about four A.M."

"You're sure? Time can be tricky when you're asleep."

"He woke me up," she said. "He came in noisy, had two straight shots, and sat awhile. Then he came and climbed all over me. The clock's right by the bed. It was almost five when he went to sleep, so it was about four when he got back."

"Does Tugela carry gambling chips? From the casino?"

"Sometimes. I've seen him playing with—"

They both heard the car coming up the muddy road in the clearing afternoon. Wood pushed the girl into the shadows behind the house. A red Impala stopped beside Virginia Gallo's green sportscar. Vinnie Tugela jumped out. Wood appeared with his suit coat open, his hand on the pistol at his belt.

"There's no creek," Wood said, "and you're not behind me."

Tugela looked at Wood, at the girl, and turned toward his car. Wood stepped closer.

"Where to?" he said.

*

Vinnie Tugela sat in the living room of the run-down farmhouse. The chaotic room of a busy bachelor, and Virginia Gallo wasn't a woman who tidied up for her men. She wasn't a woman who gave moral support, either. Wood had let her go, the green sportscar miles away already.

"I never killed Sam Garnet!" Tugela said.

"Maybe not," Wood said. "What did you do?"

"Nothing!"

Wood said, "First, you knew Sam Garnet was sneaking back into Monteverde. Second, you were watching Jitsuko Ikeda. Third, if you didn't shoot Garnet, you found his body before the motel manager did and didn't report it. Fourth, you shoved me into that locker on the *Sea King II*. That's two charges, if murder doesn't make it three."

"You slugged me on the boat! What charge is that?"

"I know Sam Garnet called some friend in Japan to find out if Jitsuko was related to Yukio Ikeda. He made that call the day Jitsuko arrived," Wood said. "The Gallo girl admits you were out in the Buick from nine that night until around four A.M. You work at that casino, carry gambling plaques. Jitsuko Ikeda saw the Buick watching the cottage at the Pearson home."

Tugela looked for a cigarette, lit it, his big arms resting on his legs as he sat forward. "Sam Garnet told me to watch the Ikeda girl until he showed up. That's all I know about it."

"Go on," Wood said.

Tugela smoked. "I drove Sam to the airport, came back here with Ginny. Sam called from L.A. about nine, gave me the number of a pay phone in his hotel. I was to tail the Ikeda girl, call him at eleven P.M. if I had her fixed. I went to the Pearson house. About ten-thirty the girl and that Pearson kid came home, went into the cottage. I had a look in the window, saw they were set for a while, you know?"

Tugela tried a grin. Wood didn't smile. Tugela shrugged. The big man went on smoking as he talked in the run-down house.

"There's a pay phone down the hill from the Pearsons. I went and called Sam at eleven. He told me to stay with the Ikeda girl. If she left the cottage, tail her, call him at the El Prado after one A.M. when I could without losing her. Using the Tracy name. If she didn't leave the cottage, I was to stay there until Garnet showed up."

"Sam Garnet was a good cop," Wood said. "A decent stake-out plan for one man."

"He was the best," Tugela said bitterly. He'd liked Sam Garnet. "Anyway, the Ikeda girl didn't even come up for air. I waited. About one A.M. the Pearson kid drove off in that Porsche. The girl was still in the cottage, so I stayed put. Alan Pearson got back about two-thirty, went in the house. Sam Garnet hadn't showed up. I waited until three A.M."

The big man's wind-creased eyes stared past Wood. "I drove to the El Prado. No one was in the office. I found out what room 'Tracy' was in. I went back. The door was open a hair, a light on. Sam Garnet was on the floor, the gun, too. I guess I bent over him, reached in my pocket for something, dropped that plaque. I don't know. Sam was dead! I'd liked him a lot, you know? Only I was scared, too. So I closed the door and beat it. I drove back here. I needed a drink, a woman."

"Why didn't you report the murder?"

"Panic, I guess. Then it was too late."

"No," Wood said. "You didn't want to be tied to what Sam Garnet had planned to do."

"I didn't know what he was going to do!"

"He had a gun, a phony name, an alibi all prepared in L.A. He was going to kill Jitsuko Ikeda."

"No!"

"He had his gun, but he wouldn't have shot her. A cop too long for that. The gun was a threat. I'd guess he planned to grab her, fake some kind of accident. No connection to him."

"You can't tie me to anything!"

"No, I can't," Wood agreed. "I can't prove what Garnet had planned, no attempt was made, and I don't think conspiracy'll stick. But I've got to know all there is if I'm going to find the killer. Garnet was your friend, you want the killer caught."

"I want it," Tugela said. "Okay, I figure he had some kind of 'accident' set for the girl. I got a hint, you know?"

"Because she was Yukio Ikeda's sister?"

"Sam said she wasn't in town just for Alan Pearson."

"So he had a friend in Japan check to be sure who she was, then planned to get rid of her. Fast, Garnet didn't take chances."

Tugela shrugged, lit another cigarette.

"Now tell me about twelve years ago," Wood said.

"I told you, I don't know nothing about then."

"Something happened to Yukio Ikeda, or Jitsuko wouldn't have been a danger to Garnet," Wood said. "Unless Garnet and Yukio Ikeda were in something illegal together, and Garnet was afraid that Jitsuko knew about it, had come to blackmail him."

"I was a kid night clerk, eighteen. I don't remember any Yukio Ikeda. Look, I told you about the other night, why would I hold back now? Would I lie if I knew anything that'd help you get Sam's killer?"

"You would if you were involved back then, too."

"I wasn't!" Tugela hunched forward. "Listen, maybe something happened twelve years ago, and maybe not. Maybe Garnet was killed because of the Ikeda girl, but maybe not, too!"

"You've got some idea about Garnet's killer?"

"I pushed you in that boat locker because George Thesiger was on the boat, hiding. He didn't want you to see him."

"Why not?"

"I don't know, but I know he's trying to take over River Enterprises. He wants to boss River awful bad, and no way with Sam Garnet around with forty percent of the stock."

"But now Alice Garnet has it."

"That's right."

"Stay put, Tugela," Wood said as he headed for the door. "Remember, we've got failing to report a murder against you, and assault on a police officer."

*

A thin afternoon sun filtered through patches of blue among the black clouds over Brandwater. James Pearson, wearing old clothes now, worked in a garden at the side of his big house. The heavy rains of the last three days had exposed rows of sprouting spring bulbs. His arms in mud up to the elbows as if he wanted to feel the dirt, delve into the earth, Pearson covered the bulbs one by one, methodically.

Jitsuko Ikeda walked across the sodden grass to stand and watch Pearson at his work. She wore a black jump suit that outlined her tiny, full body, and looked older than her nineteen years. The thoughtful, half-hidden face of a woman.

"You enjoy to work in a garden, Mr. Pearson?"

"Sometimes," Pearson said, working. "A peace to it, Suko."

"In Japan it is an art, to garden," the girl said. "You do not work in your office?"

"One of the few advantages of being president. With the rain stopped, the river is stable for the moment."

"Your wife, she is resting in the sanitarium?"

"My wife?" He looked up at the girl. "Yes, I think so."

"She will be better soon?"

"I hope so, Suko. It takes time."

"She has had many such spells?"

"Other times, yes." He stopped working. "Why, Suko?"

"I have wondered. Does she *do* things when she is sick? Bad things, perhaps? Unaware she does them?"

Pearson gently covered a bulb, its delicate green shoots just barely above the soil. "If you mean would she have done these murders, no, she wouldn't have." Pearson stood up, wiped at the mud on his arms. "You've got something on your mind?"

"I have been thinking of what that Sergeant Wood said, that Mr. Garnet was not in your company when Yukio was here twelve years ago. Mr. Garnet had not been in Japan since 1951. Yukio was only nine then. How did he know Mr. Garnet?"

"I really don't know."

"You and Mr. Garnet were on Kyushu. Yukio had never been away from Sakai, far from Kyushu. At Tanaka Instrument, he could not have learned the name of Mr. Garnet then."

"You have some point, Suko?"

"Perhaps Yukio had the name of some other person in

Monteverde. Mr. Garnet was only, what you say, an intermediary?"

"You could be right," Pearson agreed.

"I did not tell the police, but I saw someone leave Mr. Garnet's house that night. The one who searched, do you think?"

Pearson dug in the earth. "You should have told."

"It was dark, how well could I see? We are poor in Japan, and orphan most poor of all."

Pearson covered a bulb and patted the earth.

"I have thought long about Yukio," Jitsuko said. "I think he was doing something bad, and something bad happened to him."

"You thought about that before you came here?"

"Oh, yes. Poor Yukio. Still, the past may be best silent."

Pearson worked. "You think so?"

"One must live for the future."

"The future?" Pearson said, almost a question.

*

Harry Wood sat in the pale blue living room of the Thesiger house. There was a great silence in the late afternoon with the rain stopped. The rumble of the river going down. Alone, Anne Thesiger smoked.

"You never heard of Yukio Ikeda twelve years ago? You don't remember anything out of the ordinary?" Wood said.

"Nothing. Twelve years is a hell of a long time."

"Celia Pearson said nothing when you took her to Palm Springs?"

"Bitched all the way, if I know Celia. Nothing else."

"Your husband was with you all the time at the Springs?"

"My husband? George? Of course. I mean, I'm sure he was."

"Mrs. Thesiger, we know what Sam Garnet came back here under cover to do—get rid of Jitsuko Ikeda."

"You mean kill her? Sam Garnet?"

"Only someone got to him first," Wood said. "He came to kill the girl, probably because he thought she knew something. But we're not so sure that was why he was killed. Someone might have known he was back, took advantage of that to get rid of Garnet."

"Who would want to do that?" she said, smoked.

"Your husband was alone that night. He's trying to take over River Enterprises. He couldn't do that with Sam Garnet around."

"So that's what he's doing. Damn him, he—" She turned on Wood. "You're suggesting that George . . . You be careful."

"You weren't here. He wants to take over pretty bad."

"Who doesn't? But don't you try to—"

The car lurched into the driveway, hit something in a crash of metal, came to a stop with its motor still running. A car door opened, didn't close, and someone came toward the house. The front door flung open.

Anne Thesiger covered a scream.

In the doorway, George Thesiger swayed. His face, shirt and suit were a mass of blood. He breathed hoarsely, a bubbling noise in his throat. One arm hung limp. His eyes were swollen shut, his nose smashed. He took a step, almost blind.

He collapsed on the pale blue rug.

14

In the hospital room Dr. Lowell Fynn consulted in low tones with the police doctor. Anne Thesiger sat beside the bed where the battered Thesiger lay with his swollen eyes closed. Night now outside. Wood talked with the doctors.

"The X-rays are negative, no skull fracture, but he took a savage beating," the police doctor said.

"Nose broken, jaw fractured, a concussion, his left arm broken," Dr. Fynn said, the family doctor's voice shaking. "Both eyes massively bruised, he's cut up, and he lost a lot of blood."

"What did it?" Wood said.

"Fists, I'd say. Just plain fists!" Fynn said.

"Can I talk to him?"

"If he can talk, yes. He's probably in mild shock, but he's safe enough now. Nothing critical or even especially serious," Dr. Fynn said. "He'll be here a week, probably less. He's just going to hurt and look awful for quite a while."

The doctors went out into the corridor, still consulting. Before he left, Dr. Fynn patted Anne Thesiger's shoulder, comforting. Wood went to the bed. George Thesiger was breathing slowly, his eyes still closed, his good arm quiet at his side.

"Who was it, Mr. Thesiger?" Wood asked.

The beaten man seemed to cower in the bed, terror in the sound of any voice. Thesiger would remember the beating, which was what somebody wanted.

"Leave him alone!" Anne Thesiger said, a high hysteria at the edges of her voice.

Thesiger's broken jaw barely moved. Wood had to lean down, his ear close to the battered man's whisper:

"The casino . . . don't know how long . . . unconscious. They . . . the others . . . not own River . . . stay away from Alice Garnet . . ."

"Someone doesn't want you to operate River Enterprises?"

A faint nod. "Tugela . . . casino . . . stop what I . . . doing . . . Oh . . . hurt . . . hurt . . ."

"Vinnie Tugela? You can prove that?" Wood said quickly.

The faint nod. ". . . the others . . . silent partners . . . not let me . . . not good enough . . . stop . . ." One red, swollen eye opened, stared up, alarmed. Fear in the single eye. "Didn't see! . . . No . . . too dark . . . didn't see . . . who—"

"You said it was Tugela," Wood said. "We can—"

"Leave him alone!" Anne Thesiger said, pushed at Wood.

The beaten man lay breathing hard. Half in pain, and half in panic. His one eye closed again, hiding in the bed.

"Tugela'll have five good men to say he was miles away," Anne Thesiger said. "Don't you see? He doesn't want George to control River Enterprises! His money is involved, his power. He's a silent partner, maybe the whole silent thirty percent! He and Sam Garnet ran River. I should have known!"

"Who do you mean, Mrs. Thesiger?"

"My father, of course! Sam Garnet he'd trust, but not George. A danger to his interests, a threat. So he hands out a warning. Now I understand why he wants to make sure George will take a vice-president's job at Hook Instrument. He never did before, because George was just a glorified flunky for Sam Garnet, with my father behind the scenes. But George *run* River, no! Better on a vice-president's shelf under the Hook thumb!"

"River has some touchy operations," Wood said.

"And George would fight him. Poor, dumb George. All the time thinking he was independent. No one is independent of my father. His family is the world, everyone else is an alien, and *he's* the family. When his daughters needed men, he got them men—and made sure the men would stay! The money, the stock in Hook Instrument, that stayed in the girls' names! Oh, yes!"

"The men had to stay married, or lose everything?"

"Of course. My father believes in self-interest. Do a good job and be good husbands, or out on their ears. Poor George, not even aware of it. My money behind him, my position. As much a Hook slave as anyone." She looked at Thesiger silent in the bed as if trying not to be seen, noticed. "Don't talk about the family, my father said. Well, he's made a mistake!"

She lit a cigarette, smoked viciously in the silent hospital room. "You said Sam Garnet was going to get rid of that

Ikeda girl, murder her, because he was afraid she knew something about her brother? Here to blackmail Sam Garnet."

"Probably, yes."

"Which means there was something twelve years ago Sam Garnet wanted to keep hidden."

"It looks that way," Wood said.

George Thesiger stirred in the bed. Anne smoked, her eyes hard and distant.

"My sister Celia married Jim Pearson before he went off to the Korean War. A good-looking local boy without even a job. He got home once in six months, then Celia joined him in Japan. Sam Garnet was over there, too. Celia got pregnant. Her letters were happy. Twelve months later they all came home and Celia was a wreck. She'd had a miscarriage. Jim Pearson became manager of the valve department at Hook Instrument, started right up top. Sam Garnet joined the police, with my father's help. And Celia had her first breakdown in less than a year."

"You think something happened in Japan?"

"Yes, and more than a miscarriage. Celia's reaction was too much. She was always in her room, always sick, half the time under sedation. She never went out, slept apart from Jim. It was three years before Alan was born, and then she wouldn't try to handle the baby. She had her second breakdown then."

"What does it mean to you, Mrs. Thesiger?"

"That Sam Garnet was the father of that baby in Japan, of Alan, too—and Jim Pearson knew it!" She smoked fiercely. "My father paid off Jim Pearson with Hook Instrument's best product to manage, a straight road to the presidency. Jim's played the good husband ever since. My father made it worthwhile for Sam Garnet, too. So Celia could have her lover on the sly."

In the bed, George Thesiger moaned weakly, as if trying to protest. His one eye opened, but only stared up vacant.

Wood said, "Did your sister have a breakdown in March, 1962? Not just a vacation in Palm Springs?"

"No, but Celia was nervous, I remember. Maybe Jim Pearson sent her away before anything could happen. Yukio Ikeda must have known about Celia and Garnet, and something happened to him."

"You think Sam Garnet killed Yukio Ikeda twelve years ago?" Wood said. "But who killed Garnet now? Why?"

Anne Thesiger said nothing.

"Other people could have wanted to protect Celia's name," Wood said. "Yukio Ikeda might have talked to others besides Sam Garnet. Maybe even Alan."

"Alan? He was seven years old then."

"Kids can pull triggers," Wood said. "Murder is a drastic solution just to hide adultery. Or even that Alan is Garnet's son, not Pearson's."

"Perhaps it was half an accident," Anne Thesiger said. She looked at her silent husband. "Or perhaps something else happened in Japan. Something worse than adultery and a miscarriage."

Anne Thesiger's fierce eyes looked straight at Wood. In the bed George Thesiger moaned again, began to thrash. Anne went to him, calmed him. Wood went out.

*

In the hospital corridor, Wood found Dr. Lowell Fynn. Fynn was an older man in a dark suit and vest, with a rimless pince-nez hanging down on a black ribbon.

"Are you Celia Pearson's doctor, too, Dr. Fynn?"

"I am, Sergeant. All her life, just about."

"Can we talk a minute?"

Dr. Fynn hesitated. "Very well, come along."

In a doctors' lounge, Dr. Fynn locked the door, began to polish his pince-nez.

Wood said, "Was Celia Pearson pregnant in Japan twenty-three years ago?"

"Yes, she was."

"Was she pregnant before she was married?"

"No, she was not." Dr. Fynn polished his pince-nez. The habit of a man who needs to keep his hands busy at difficult moments. "Celia was a month pregnant when she went to Japan. She went there to be with Jim. He was stationed in a quiet village on special duty at the time. An ideal place."

"What happened to the baby?"

"Miscarriage. In her sixth month, nasty. She had a breakdown, Jim Pearson took her to a sanitarium in Los Angeles."

"When they got home then, was Sam Garnet with them?"

"Are you listening to rumors, Sergeant?"

"Why wouldn't she care for Alan as a baby?"

"A delicate woman, highly neurotic. She feared for the child. Sergeant, Celia's had four psychotic episodes, counting the first in Japan and this new one."

"What causes them, Doctor? When was the last before now?"

"The last was when Alan was born. We've been lucky. They are brought on by tense conflict. The base cause we

122

don't know."

"Nineteen years until now? Was she always so sick?"

"Not as bad. She became much worse after her miscarriage. It happens to some women," Dr. Fynn said. "As for the nineteen years, Celia has lesser spells every year or so, we never know. She visits the sanitarium often for treatment, but has not been committed for extensive care since Alan's birth."

"On tenterhooks, but not over the edge in a long time, Doc?"

"You could say that."

"When did she go to Japan? The exact date?"

"You mean twenty-three years ago? I'd have to check."

"I'd appreciate it," Wood said.

*

Wood had some dinner, and it was past nine P.M. when he got back to his desk this time. A message was there from Dr. Fynn.

Celia Pearson had gone to Japan in December, 1950. She had come back to Monteverde in early January, 1952. That meant her miscarriage would have been in late May, 1951, and she would have left Japan and gone into the L.A. sanitarium probably in June, 1951. Wood picked up his telephone, called Dr. Fynn.

"What was the name of the village in Japan where Pearson and Sam Garnet were stationed?"

"It was called Uta-Kaze, on Kyushu."

Wood wrote out a cable, sent it off to the Osaka police again. Then he went to the old personnel files of the department. He found Sam Garnet's file. Garnet had come home to Monteverde in January, 1952, also. It proved nothing. Yet?

If Celia Pearson had been in a sanitarium all those months, Jim Pearson would be expected to stay near her. But where had Sam Garnet been? Near her, too?

*

Alice Garnet stood framed in the light of her doorway. The night seemed strange without rain.

"I've got some coffee ready," Alice said.

She was wearing black.

"The funeral's tomorrow," she said.

She poured coffee for Wood, and a brandy. He took both. They sat on the couch.

"I don't even want to go," she said. "To the funeral. Sam was a solitary boy, and a solitary man. Like our father. My father was a man who believed all the success myths, work hard and get ahead. When he didn't get anywhere, he began to hate. But he didn't hate poverty, he just hated being poor. He didn't hate the rich, he wanted to be one of them. Sam grew up like him. I don't think Sam ever had a thought not about himself."

"What about you?" Wood said.

"Me? I hope I'm better, Harry."

Wood told her about the beating of George Thesiger.

"Seems he wants to run River. Did he come to you, Alice?"

She nodded. "Yes, he wanted an option and my proxy."

"Were you going to give them to him?"

"I haven't given it a lot of thought yet."

"Anyone else approach you?"

"No, not yet."

"You think Thesiger could have killed Sam? For his chance?"

"He could have, I guess. Seized an opportunity." She drank her brandy. "Maybe it's all something Sam had even forgotten, from far back."

"A cop's life? Long hours, bad pay, and a bullet?"

"Bullets can be waiting for anyone. One kind of bullet or another. It's necessary work, we need it."

"You don't think it's such a bad life?"

"No," she said. "Your cup's empty."

She went into the kitchen to pour the coffee, her body soft in the black dress, her hair redder. She sat beside him again. Wood told her what Anne Thesiger had said about Garnet and Celia.

"You're sure Sam wasn't mixed up with Celia Pearson?"

"As sure as I can be," Alice said. "Anne Thesiger always was jealous of Celia and Jim Pearson."

"Could Celia have had some other man?"

"Monteverde's a small town, and Celia was odd after Japan. I was only fifteen, but I remember Jim Pearson going everywhere alone. I used to be sorry for Jim. Sometimes, they'd be out together, and Celia'd just get up and leave. But who?"

A clock struck somewhere. Ten o'clock. There was laughter out in the night, and a car door slammed in the distance.

"I better go," Wood said. He stood up.

She looked up at him. "After the murderer? On the trail?"

"I guess so."

"The funeral depresses me," she said. "I've been thinking about what you said, about leaving Monteverde."

"Why not wait a while?" Wood said.

She nodded. "Harry? Stay with me tonight."

He sat down again. She leaned close against him. When he picked her up to carry her into the bedroom, she clung to him.

15

Captain Vause was at Wood's desk the next morning. The wall clock read nine-forty.

"Banker's hours?" Vause said. He wasn't smiling.

Wood had been feeling good. A nice night, and a pleasant breakfast. Vause took it all away.

"Ready to take me off the case?" Wood said. "Hoag, old Hook, maybe the mayor on your neck?"

Vause flushed. "Maybe I should! What've you done?"

"You heard about George Thesiger? Want me to arrest old Hook? I've got an accusation against him. Or maybe I should pick up Alan Pearson? His car was seen at Roberta Dunn's house the night she was killed."

Vause was silent. "You talk to the boy?"

"I don't think he'd drive that Porsche to murder anyone," Wood said. "He could have come back, but I want to know more."

"Okay," Vause said. "Sorry, Harry. You handle it." The Captain chewed a fingernail. "You really think Cornelius Hook had Thesiger beaten up? Thesiger said so?"

"Anne Thesiger says so," Wood said. "Don't worry, Captain, Thesiger isn't going to talk about it. He was warned, and he'll take the hint. Hook's safe, unless I can make Tugela talk."

"Is the beating part of the murders?"

"Indirectly. Any closer I don't know yet," Wood said. "You sure you want to know any closer?"

Vause got up. "I live with these people, Harry. I like them. But I want the answers."

The Captain stalked away. Wood sat down. He was being unfair to Vause. Maybe no better than most men, but so far a good cop. The old saw—the police are no better than the community they serve. Old but true. Not the community itself, but the "climate" it moved in, the tone set by its leaders. Why should anyone expect a cop to be more honest or moral than a rich man?

Wood saw the cable on his desk. From Japan. Mrs. and Lt. Pearson had left Uta-Kaze, and Japan, in July, 1951. That fitted. But there was no record of a miscarriage or a breakdown in any hospital on Kyushu or anywhere else in Japan.

*

Sandbags were piled ten high around all the buildings of Hook Instrument Company. The yards were dry, but the river still ran high. No rain, but no sun either. Clouds on the far mountains.

James Pearson was in the plant. Wood found him in a dim corner of a production building. The machines operated noisily, but many workers were still moving materiel to high trestles. James Pearson wore rubber boots, directed the workers. He had his jacket off, color in his face as if enjoying the work.

"Can it possibly wait, Sergeant?" he said, called out orders.

"I'll follow along. You know about George Thesiger?"
"I heard, yes."
"You believe what Mrs. Thesiger is saying about Mr. Hook?"

Pearson took hold of an end of a heavy box with a worker, heaved it up onto a trestle.

"My father-in-law is a man who knows what must be done." Pearson brushed his hands together. "He has the largest silent share in River Enterprises. Garnet voted his share. Now—?"

"You have any interest in River?"

"Yes, a small one. Sam Garnet voted mine, too."

"Your wife once had a miscarriage in Japan, Mr. Pearson?"

Pearson watched his workers carrying the bags and boxes up to the high trestles, stacking them in case the rain returned. He rubbed at his eyes as if not seeing well in the dim interior.

Wood said, "I cabled Japan. No record of her miscarriage in Uta-Kaze, or in Japan. You left Japan in July, 1951, and your wife wasn't due until August."

James Pearson watched his men for another moment, then went to a shop bench and sat down.

"We told everyone that Celia had miscarried to avoid worse explanations. My wife was very sick when we came home."

"What really happened?"

Pearson sighed. "Celia became afraid to have the baby in Japan. We returned to a private clinic in Los Angeles. There were complications, the baby was born dead. Celia blamed herself. She blamed her fear for killing the child. I mean, she had been afraid to risk the birth in Japan, and when the baby died anyway, she was sure it would have lived if she *had* had it in Japan, you see? Irrational."

Pearson's handsome face was drawn. Pain in his cloudy eyes. He watched the men lifting the heavy boxes as if thinking about his child who had never had a chance to lift anything.

"She'd be twenty-three, our first child. Celia's never really accepted it. She celebrates Sarah's birthday in secret, not aware I know. She even buys presents. Do you wonder why we told the miscarriage story?"

"No," Wood said.

Pearson seemed to see the years among the noisy machines of his factory. "I was busy starting a career. But that wasn't it. We were young, and I was a nurse, not a husband. Not that I blamed Celia, she had to be protected. After Alan was born—" He shook invisible cobwebs from his face, his eyes. "That was the last time, we began to think. But it's still all with us. Sometimes I wonder if it could have been different, if I could have changed any of it. If I'd tried more, done things differently."

"What shook her this time? Jitsuko Ikeda?"

"Partly. A young girl from Japan, you see?"

"The girl herself, Mr. Pearson, or her name?"

"Name?" Pearson didn't seem to understand.

"Ikeda, like Yukio. Sam Garnet recognized the name."

"Celia never heard of Yukio Ikeda."

"Did you, then? Twelve years ago?"

Pearson shook his head. His hands fluttered vaguely.

"We think Sam Garnet came back to murder Jitsuko Ikeda," Wood said. "Because she was Yukio Ikeda's sister."

"No," Pearson said. "I mean . . . I can't believe that."

"Where were you that night, Mr. Pearson? At home?"

"No, I was out. Celia was . . . resting. I was out most of that night. At the country club later. Until one-fifteen or so. The club bar closes at one A.M. I left a bit later."

"When did you get home?"

Pearson blinked. "I looked in on Celia, I remember. She was sleeping. It was about two A.M., I'm sure. Before two."

"Did she see you? Or anyone else? Alan, maybe?"

"No. Didn't Alan say he was out until two-thirty or so?"

"Yeh, he did. You were out when Roberta Dunn was shot, too?"

"At the plant here. The rain, you see? We were working."

"But people saw you that evening?"

"There was a lot of confusion. I'm not sure."

"Your son visited Miss Dunn the night she died?"

"Yes, he and Jitsuko. They left at six o'clock."

"Where were they after six?"

Pearson frowned. "I think you should ask them."

"You've talked to them, Mr. Pearson. I'll ask later."

"Jitsuko was in the cottage. Alan was out for dinner."

"What about your wife?"

"Celia was in her room."

"Alone? Only you saw her at home when Garnet was shot?"

"I saw her, Sergeant. Sleeping."

"I'll have to talk to her, Mr. Pearson."

Pearson was shocked. "But you can't! No."

"Sorry. Sick people sometimes do things, Mr. Pearson."

Pearson was silent, watched his workers, shook his head.

"I'll have to go to her without you," Wood said.

Pearson sat for a time. He listened to the noise of his

production machines the way other men listen to music.

"I'd rather be there. The shock will be less."

*

On the freeway, neither man spoke. The creeks flowed steadily under the bridges. The sea was still rough, the sky dark. They passed through San Vicente and on out of Buena Costa County. The land flattened into truck farms and lemon groves, ugly towns half Mexican with the imported lemon pickers. They climbed up into the mountains toward Los Angeles before James Pearson spoke.

"I built Hook Instrument. Doubled its business. Took a small company and made it a solid factor in the industry. I don't apologize for that. I did it."

"Why should you apologize?" Wood said.

"What?" Pearson said. "Why should I? Accidents happen, but life has to go on. You can't just hide, miss out."

Pearson stared ahead. Just past the Topanga Canyon exit, he directed Wood off onto Ventura Boulevard. They turned east into the foothills. The sanitarium was a mile into the hills.

It stood behind a high iron fence, its lawn as smooth as a golf green. Patients wandered in the gray day. Wood parked in the visitors' lot, and a brisk doctor in a white coat greeted Pearson in his office. The doctor was professionally cheerful, but his eyes were tight and his windows were barred.

"I think we can hope for a quick recovery this time," the doctor said, "but no visitors except you just yet, Mr. Pearson."

"Sergeant Wood is a police detective," Pearson said.

"Out of the question."

"It's a murder case, Doctor," Wood said.

"Her testimony couldn't be used in court, Sergeant. No—"

"I know that. I can get a court order."

Pearson said, "I'll be with him, Doctor."

"Well—?" The doctor looked at Pearson. "Very well."

They went along three corridors to a door with a glass judas window. The doctor unlocked the door. They went in. James Pearson put on a broad smile.

"How are you, Celia?" Pearson said.

16

On a sunny day it would have been a pleasant room. No padding, and no bars. Like a well-furnished sitting room. But the windows were all high, the furniture was bolted down, there was nothing small and movable, and the day was gray.

"Celia?" Pearson said again.

She sat in an armchair with her hands loose in her lap. Her thin face seemed longer and thinner, her nose curved sharp, her cheeks hollow, and her eyes fixed on space. The thick, dark hair had been pulled back and held not with a ribbon but with a rubber band. Her tall body jutted against the cloth of her black dress.

"Your husband is here, Mrs. Pearson," the doctor said.

She looked toward Pearson. "Of course. How are you, dear?"

"I'm fine, Celia. Are you—?"

She looked at Wood. "I'm sorry, I know I forget people when I'm . . . when I'm—?" She wrinkled her brow as if trying to remember what she was when she forgot people.

"Sergeant Wood, Mrs. Pearson."

"Sergeant? My husband was a lieutenant. In Japan. That was . . . a few years ago."

"I'm a policeman, not a soldier, Mrs. Pearson. Are you afraid of the police? Worried?"

"In Japan," she said. "A terrible place. Terrible—!" She looked at Pearson, smiled. "I'm much better, dear. Oh, yes."

Pearson held her hand. Wood took the doctor aside.

"How much can she remember, Doctor?"

"Almost impossible to tell. I warned you. Recent events, she's almost certain not to remember. The more distant events will be erratic, haphazard. Out of time."

Wood turned back to the Pearsons. Celia smiled at him again. A polite smile, social, as if she were a hostess at some event where she knew it was proper to be warm to strangers. Pearson spoke gently to his wife, clinging to her hand.

"Sergeant Wood wants to ask some questions, Celia. If you can't remember, we'll all understand."

"Questions?" Her eyes alert. "That sounds nice."

Wood said, "Did you like Sam Garnet, Mrs. Pearson?"

James Pearson's hand whitened on his wife's hand. She made a noise, pulled her hand away, shook her head at Pearson for hurting her. She folded her hands, smiled at Wood.

"Sam Garnet? Should I? Yes, I can feel I know him—!"

"Years ago," Wood said. "In Japan. You liked Garnet."

"Japan?" Her face twisted, like a different face. Then, "Oh, Jimmy's friend! The military police officer. I . . . I don't really like him. No, a crude man, rough. Not . . . but Jimmy's friend, of course. Too rough, he doesn't understand."

"Twelve years ago a man came to your house. Yukio Ikeda. Only a boy," Wood said. "One night in March twelve years ago. You remember him. Yukio Ikeda."

"Wood—!" Pearson began, his voice strained.

The doctor silenced Pearson with a sharp wave. The danger was tension, confusion. Celia Pearson was unconcerned, serene.

"The girl, yes. Jitsuko Ikeda. Alan's young lady. Alan and Ikeda, I remember."

"Your son Alan saw Yukio Ikeda at your house?" Wood said.

Her face went limp as if the bones and muscles were jelly. "A boy this time! I won't look!" She dropped her voice to a whisper. "Is he . . . is he . . . all right? No! I . . . I can't! I won't—" She shook her head violently. "What? You said Ikeda? Japanese! A pretty girl, so pretty. She . . . she died. Yes, died!"

Wood said, "Who died, Mrs. Pearson? Yukio Ikeda? Twelve years ago? Someone—?"

"Sarah died! You know that! She's dead . . . dead—!"

The tears seemed to spurt down her thin, wasted face. No violence, only the tears and a face twenty years older than it should have been. Pearson held her close, leaned her face against his chest. He was oblivious to Wood, to the doctor. Whispering low to his wife, softly, steadily.

"It's enough, Sergeant Wood," the doctor said.

Wood watched the crying woman. Not hysterical, only sitting there with her face against Pearson, and the tears pouring down like water almost without emotion. Water or blood, from some unseen wound.

Wood left the room. The doctor came behind him. Pearson remained holding his wife.

*

The doctor sat at his desk. "Well, what did you learn?"

"I wanted reaction," Wood said. "Something."

"Did you get it? You can't trust her answers."

"I've seen her. I'll have to learn more."

"Is that all here, then?"

"No," Wood said. "She came here first twenty-three years ago. Tell me why, and when, and where she came from."

"I wasn't here twenty-three years ago, Sergeant."

"The sanitarium was. There must be records."

The doctor's face said he would have liked to throw Wood out. But sanitariums were a delicate business, too full of charlatans. The doctor made a phone call, sat back.

"Is she aware of what she does now?" Wood asked.

"Sometimes. Her state is unpredictable. She could act quite normal, or totally deranged. She might or might not know what she was doing in both cases. She could be unable to put on a shoe without forgetting what she was doing or how to do it, or she could fix on some action and follow it all the way no matter how intricate."

"What triggers these spells? Her smaller nervousness?"

"Some intolerable conflict inside her."

"Her dead daughter?"

"That's clearly a major cause, a basis in her past. But in the present, no one can say just what might trigger an episode."

"Some violent action? Something she did?"

"That could do it, the guilt, need to hide from herself," the doctor said. "But a sudden memory would do it, too. Anything that caused her to remember what she wants to forget. Any incident that makes her chronic neurosis acute."

An attendant came in with a folder. The doctor opened the folder. Wood made no attempt to look at it; he had no warrant. He hoped the doctor wouldn't be difficult.

The doctor read aloud, "She was first admitted on September 12, 1951—psychotic episode, or nervous breakdown to you. Discharged January 9, 1952. Re-admitted on May 4, 1953, same cause, and discharged on July 19, 1953. Once more on January 28, 1955, until April 14, 1955. Same diagnosis, her son had been born. That was the last admission until now, but she came as an outpatient many times between."

"Not in March, 1962? You're sure?"

The doctor read. "No, not even as an outpatient."

"What does it say about the first admission?"

"She'd had a child that died."

"Where was the child born?"

"The record doesn't say. But she had been a patient in Mountain View Clinic prior to coming here."

Wood thought about the dates. Japan, children, and maybe Sam Garnet? The date of the second admission was after Japan and the dead baby, and before Alan. Something was missing.

"Where is this Mountain View Clinic?" Wood asked.

"That can't help you. It closed down fifteen years ago."

"Its records should be somewhere."

"Yes, I suppose they are."

Wood went to the door. "Tell Pearson I'll be back."

*

Lieutenant Carl Rudi, L.A.P.D., had once worked with Wood on a missing persons case. Rudi listened to Wood's story, then made a phone call. It took a half hour.

"Mountain View Clinic closed down all right, Harry. Patients and records transferred to Valley Extended-Care. That's in North Hollywood."

"Let's go there," Wood said.

They drove through the Hollywood Hills past Universal City to a complex of low stucco buildings in a brown valley. The medical record librarian was a woman in her sixties.

"Yes, we have Mountain View's records."

Wood and Carl Rudi followed the librarian to a crowded storage room. She dug among piles of boxes and storage files until she found a dusty stack that hadn't been touched in years. She pointed to the P box. Wood dragged it out. The librarian went through it.

"Here we are," the librarian said. "Pearson, Mrs. Celia. Maternity patient. Admitted August 22, 1951. An extended labor, but a normal birth on August 26, 1951. There seem to have been some complications, but Mrs. Pearson was in good condition."

"The child?"

"A girl, seven pounds, six ounces. Name—" the librarian clucked, turned a page. "That's odd, there's no data on the child. The record stops at the bottom of a page."

"Could there be a page missing?"

"The last page is full. Still, there's no doctor's signature. That's not too unusual, I'm afraid. Doctors hate to do charts, and a private clinic can be terribly sloppy."

"Would there be a separate chart on the baby?"

"Possibly. You know the child's name?"

"Sarah."

The librarian went through the file. "No chart here for Sarah Pearson. It could have been sent somewhere."

"There'd be a notation, wouldn't there?" Lieutenant Rudi said.

"There should be. Those private clinics are careless, and some data may have been lost in transfer."

Wood said, "Look for a chart for Sarah Garnet."

The librarian did. "No, there's no Sarah Garnet, either."

All the way back to Carl Rudi's office, Wood thought about the missing records. If they were missing. When they were in Rudi's office, he asked Rudi to check city records for birth and death certificates.

"Try Pearson, Garnet and Hook," Wood said. "Sarah on all."

It took an hour.

"Birth certificate on Sarah Pearson," Rudi reported. "Born, August 26, 1951. Mother: Celia Hook Pearson. Father: James Donald Pearson. Mountain View Clinic. All okay."

"Death certificate?"

"None, Harry. I guess she didn't die in Los Angeles."

"Or the death wasn't reported."

"Deaths have to be reported."

"I know," Wood said.

He drove back to the sanitarium. The doctor was at work in his office.

"Mr. Pearson had to leave, Sergeant. He rented a car."

"Where did he go?"

"He didn't tell me."

In his car, Wood drove north. The sky was all black. It began to rain again before he was five miles out of Los Angeles.

*

In his raincoat, James Pearson dripped water onto the rug in Cornelious Hook's glass-walled study.

"Wood talked to Celia?" Cornelius Hook said.

"She wasn't rational, said nothing," Pearson said.

Pearson watched the new rain, and Vaal Creek below

Hook's glass wall of windows as if he wondered what he was doing in this house at all. A sense of aimlessness, futility, a circle in which he ran around and around.

"But Wood asked about Mountain View," he said. "A stubborn man, he'll find out. Celia couldn't face that."

"You're sure, Jim? Perhaps she could after all," old Hook said, his owl-face alert. "It's not too late."

"She'd go insane, totally. I've always known that, tried to shield her. I did try, Cornelius."

"I know you did," Hook said.

"I tried to stop it this time. No more."

"Maybe that was wrong. You should have talked to me."

"You?" Pearson looked out and down at Vaal Creek as if he wanted to step into the deep, clear water. "I listened to you, didn't I? I listened to too many people. I wonder if I should have listened to myself? I wonder if there's still a chance if I listen to myself, try it my way? What I want?"

"There's always a chance, Jim," old Hook said. "Sit down, we'll talk it out. This Wood—"

"Talk? No, I don't think so."

Pearson left a trail of dark water as he left the study. Cornelius Hook listened to his outside door close.

17

By the time Harry Wood crossed the Buena Costa County line, the rain was so heavy it bounced off the freeway in geysers, and in San Vicente the main creek was over its banks. In Monteverde, the Santa Rosa River boiled along the sandbag levee, the city lighted in midafternoon as if it were night.

In Brandwater they were evacuating low-lying houses along Vaal Creek. The big Pearson house was safe on its hill. There was light in the house, and Alan Pearson's white Porsche was parked at the garage. A red Jaguar was inside the garage. Wood didn't see any rental car.

Alan Pearson answered the door.

"Your father here?" Wood asked.

"No. His office said he'd gone to L.A. with you."

"He left L.A. Rented a car. The housekeeper around?"

"Her sister lives on the river; she went to help."

The thin boy took Wood back into a large kitchen. Jitsuko Ikeda was making a pot of tea. Slim in a dark green Chinese dress, she looked at Wood, got out a third cup. Wood drank the tea; it had been a long, raw drive in the new rain.

"You two went to see Roberta Dunn the night she was shot?"

"Yes, but we left at six," Alan said. "Maybe if—?"

"But you could have gone back, both of you?"

"I could," Alan said, "not Suko. She had no car."

"Cars can be rented and hidden," Wood said. The tea was hot and good. "You're sure neither of you did go back?"

"No, we didn't!"

"Miss Ikeda?" Wood said.

"I did not go back," the girl said.

Alan said, "But I think Miss Dunn *did* know something, Sergeant. I think she saw Yukio Ikeda with Sam Garnet twelve years ago, and maybe with someone else, too. Or heard something."

"I wonder if she knew something more recent?" Wood said. He finished his tea, put down the cup. "We're pretty sure why Sam Garnet was back in Monteverde—to arrange an 'accident' for Miss Ikeda there. A fatal accident."

"You mean . . . ? Kill Suko?" Alan cried.

The girl said, her voice shaky, "Mr. Garnet wished me dead?"

"He'd already checked in Japan to make sure you were Yukio's sister, had a man named Tugela watching you in that Buick. He was afraid of you, Miss Ikeda. Probably afraid you'd come here to blackmail. You didn't come to blackmail, did you?"

"Of course she didn't!" Alan said.

"Jitsuko?" Wood said.

"I came to learn about my brother," Jitsuko said. Her voice dropped low. "Perhaps to make someone pay if . . . if—"

Her voice faded away. Alan Pearson watched his teacup.

"Maybe you talked to Sam Garnet privately," Wood said. "You were in his house the night he was shot. Had he let you know something about Yukio? You went to that motel? Maybe Roberta Dunn wasn't all finished with Garnet, saw you at the motel."

The girl seemed to shrink. "I did not talk to him, I did not go to that motel. I was going to talk to him . . . later."

Alan said, "You think Sam Garnet did know what happened to Yukio Ikeda, and that's why he was scared of Suko?"

Wood nodded. "He either thought she knew, or just being around to ask questions was enough. That Jitsuko was here in town was enough. Sam Garnet didn't run risks he could help."

There was a silence in the big kitchen, the rain loud on the metal gutters and the stone terrace outside.

"What I wonder is what Yukio Ikeda came here for twelve years ago? A money project." Wood lit a cigarette. "Alan, did you know your mother never did have a miscarriage?"

"Mother? But, she did! We all know that."

"No. She had the baby, but it died. In L.A., not Japan."

"Died? Then what's the difference?"

"I'm afraid there's a hell of a lot of difference," Wood said. "A baby's a person, and when a person dies, there has to be a death certificate. There isn't one, Alan. Not in L.A."

Jitsuko said, "What does that mean Sergeant?"

"That her death wasn't in L.A., or wasn't reported."

The girl said, "Why would her death not be reported?"

"Yeh, why?" Wood said. "Unless someone didn't want

her death known. Didn't want a doctor or cop to see her."

Alan gripped a table. "You mean you think my mother—?"

"I don't know what I think yet, or about who," Wood said. "What did Yukio Ikeda come here to do twelve years ago? What did he know that was worth money?"

Jitsuko Ikeda sat down, shook her head. Alan seemed to listen to the rain. Wood went to the door.

"If you see your father, call me."

*

Alice Garnet wasn't at her apartment. Wood drove downtown to the advertising agency where she worked. Traffic was a massive snarl, fire and police vehicles swarming through the city as the sandbag levee threatened to give way under the new torrent.

Alice was alone in the office, dressed in black, bent over a drawing board under a cone of light. A hat with a black veil was beside her. Wood had forgotten the funeral of Sam Garnet.

"Everyone's out saving the family silver," Alice said as Wood came in. "People love emergencies, excites them."

"How about some coffee?" Wood said.

They went through the rain to The Dregs coffee house. A businessman was talking to the manager about the floods. The manager pointed to a bearded artist who had had his shack and all he owned washed away. The artist was reading a book of Zen. Wood told Alice about his trip to Los Angeles with Pearson.

"That's why he missed the funeral," she said. "He must be frantic about Celia to forget. The poor child died, Harry?"

"Twenty-three years ago. But not in Los Angeles. Unless they hid her death."

"Hid?"

Wood warmed his hands on his coffee cup. "Maybe they didn't want anyone to know how she died, Alice."

"Not want . . .? Oh, no, Harry! That's horrible! No!"

"If she died in the clinic at birth, there'd be a death certificate. It couldn't have been lost or stolen, it'd be on file, and why take the records? But if the baby had died somewhere else, unreported, then stealing the records would cover. Except, then, why leave Celia's record to show the birth?"

Wood stirred his coffee. "Sam came home in January, 1952. So did the Pearsons, but they'd been in the States since July, 1951. Where was Sam from July, 1951, to January, 1952?"

"In Japan, as far as I know. In Uta-Kaze. Jim Pearson had special leave to bring Celia home after her trouble. So we heard."

"Alice? What if Sam *was* the child's father? Jim Pearson found out. Or Celia knew, was afraid—"

"Harry, don't!"

"Alice, Sam was murdered. Roberta Dunn, who knew him and the Pearsons, was murdered. Yukio Ikeda, from Japan with some scheme to get rich, vanished. Why all the rumors, and where was Sam while Celia Pearson was in that sanitarium?"

"The rumors started because Celia shut Pearson out, Harry. He was always alone, and this is a small town," Alice said. "I'm sure Sam was still in Uta-Kaze. I remember letters about the fishing. It's a little fishing village, he loved it there. The war was almost over, he had little to do. I know—"

"Why the miscarriage lie? Why say it was in Japan, not

in Los Angeles? To keep people far from some truth? What did Yukio Ikeda expect to make money on? Why no death certificate?"

"I don't know, Harry. Perhaps the child didn't even die! I mean, not then. Later, older, and not in Los Angeles. Celia—"

Wood had stopped listening. Alice Garnet trailed off, she watched Wood. He was sitting as if watching the bearded artist and his book of Zen. Then Wood's eyes closed for a moment.

"Harry?" Alice said.

Wood held up his hand. "Wait. Maybe . . . I remember now, I read something. It could be, but . . . Stay here—" Wood opened his eyes. "No, go home. I'm going back to L.A. Go home."

Alice Garnet sat alone for some time after Wood had gone.

*

Alice Garnet closed her door, leaned against it. She looked around her small apartment as if wondering what to do next. A public event, the funeral, for the vice-president. The important man. Poor Sam, he'd liked all that so damned much.

She took off her hat and coat, shook her copper hair loose. She looked at herself in her mirror. There was some money, was there time for more than that? She smiled. A cop? She stopped smiling and looked at her telephone.

She poured herself a brandy, drank, and looked toward her telephone again. She was still standing over the phone when someone came up the walk toward her door. The knock was heavy, not Wood's knock. Alice opened her door slowly.

"Good afternoon, Alice," Cornelius Hook said.

"If you want Jim Pearson, he isn't here, Mr. Hook," Alice said.

"Is Sergeant Wood here?"

"No," she said.

"Then may I come in, Alice?" old Hook said.

She walked back into her small living room. Hook closed the door behind him. The heavy old man was massive in the room. He glanced around, his face showing nothing, and sat down.

"You like Sergeant Wood, Alice?" Hook said.

"You don't miss a lot, do you, Mr. Hook?"

"It doesn't pay to be surprised."

She drank her brandy. "You're never surprised?"

"I hope not often."

"Not even by George Thesiger?"

"I admit that did catch me short. Who would have thought George had the gumption. Possibly even more than we know, eh?" Hook sat with his hands in his broad lap. "I'm actually unhappy about George, but a man shouldn't play over his head. He'll be all right. He'll be a vice-president at Hook Instrument, Anne will be mollified. I'll pay him well for his share of River Enterprises, find someone to run it who can make us both rich. Or I'll offer better than top dollar for your share."

"What does Vinnie Tugela get?"

"The boat, a promotion."

"You said *better* than top dollar for my share? Just how far over his head had George Thesiger played, Mr. Hook?"

"I don't know, and I don't want to. But I see you get the point. Sam is buried, why not leave him in peace, eh?"

Alice finished her brandy. "What do you want, Mr. Hook?"

"To protect my family, of course."

"Do they have to be protected?"

"That's something else I don't want to know," Hook said. "But one of them might have to be. You understand me?"

Alice Garnet sat down. Then she got up again, went and poured more brandy. She returned to her couch without offering Cornelius Hook a brandy. She sat with the snifter in both hands.

"You know where Sergeant Wood is now, Alice?" Hook said.

"Yes. On his way to Los Angeles. He was there today, saw Celia, found out about the child who died. He wondered why he found no death certificate. I think he's gone with some idea."

"So he thought of that, did he. A smart man, and thorough. All right, that can't be helped. But—"

Alice said, "What happened to that child, Mr. Hook?"

"I'm afraid he'll find out," Hook said. "You like Wood, Alice. Does he like you? A lot?"

"Why?"

"He's almost forty, still a sergeant. He has no capital, not much future. I'd like to bribe him, stop all the trouble in my family. He might be more ready to accept if you went with the money. A full life."

"Why would I want to help you? You think I'd sell—"

"Not me, Alice," Hook said. "Call it a clean slate. Wood gets money and you. You get him, top price for your holdings. All he does is fail. Nothing positive, just an unsolved case. I'm not sure it can be solved anyway. I haven't a clue."

"Wood won't do it," Alice said.

"He just might if you make it worth his while. A new life somewhere else. You always wanted to leave Monteverde."

"He won't solve it in Los Angeles?"

"No, I don't think so."

"Was Sam really going to kill that girl?"

"I expect he was. Sam was like that—direct." Hook stood up. "I think you'd regret not trying with Wood, Alice."

The old man nodded to her and crossed to the door and out in his rolling walk. Alice Garnet sat alone with her brandy.

18

The sanitarium grounds were rain-swept and deserted when Wood drove in. The doctor stood up as Wood entered his office.

"Has Pearson come back?" Wood said.

"Not since you left. If you want to talk to Mrs. Pearson again, Sergeant, I have to say no."

Wood sat down. "I don't want to talk to Mrs. Pearson."

"Then what do you want? I'm a busy man, this isn't your jurisdiction."

"Call Lieutenant Rudi then. You want his number?"

The doctor sat down.

"We located Mountain View Clinic's records. Sarah Pearson was born in the clinic. Birth certificate checks, but it seems the child's records are missing, and we couldn't find any death certificate at all."

"It must be somewhere else, another county."

Wood said, "Something came to me, Doctor. An article I'd read in a magazine about a fishing village in Japan. I stopped in the library on my way here."

"I see," the doctor said.

"Is that why all the lies? Mrs. Pearson's chronic illness,

her breakdowns? No death certificate?"

"I'm sorry, Sergeant, I haven't the authority—"

Wood said, "I think Sarah Pearson is a motive in two murders. I can go to an L.A. judge, make it public, nothing the Pearsons could do."

"I suppose you could."

"Do you know where Sarah is, Doctor?"

"Yes," the doctor said. "She's here."

Wood waited. The doctor got up reluctantly.

"I suppose you want to see her?"

Wood followed the doctor out of the office and along the corridors. There were no distant screams or manic laughter, the sanitarium quiet. The doctor took Wood to a wing on the other side of the sanitarium from Celia Pearson's room. Therapy rooms opened off the dim corridor. The doctor stopped at a door.

"You're sure, Sergeant?" he said.

"Yes," Wood said.

The doctor opened the door, stepped back. Wood looked into the room. It was a bare, narrow room with nothing but a bed and a single night light. Sarah Pearson lay on the bed under only a sheet. Very small for twenty-three. She heard Wood and the doctor. Her face moved, directionless like an insect.

"She's deformed, spastic, mute and blind," the doctor said. "Totally crippled, can't control her movements or speak. A vegetable since she was born. Mercury poisoning in the womb."

Wood turned from the open door. He leaned with his hands flat on the corridor wall, his head down. He breathed deeply.

The doctor closed the door. "They brought Sarah here

when she was born. Celia Pearson had collapsed. She couldn't accept it, or even face it. She never really has faced it. She didn't want it known, was afraid to have another child for years, was afraid to look at Alan when he was born. Irrational, Alan was fine, but a real fear. Perhaps the poison affected her a little, too. It's capricious, strikes some, not others. The degree varies. Unborn infants are especially vulnerable."

"That was in the article," Wood said, his head still down, his breathing slow and deep. "Uta-Kaze sickness."

"A hundred-and-seventy victims in Uta-Kaze out of three thousand people, all fishing people," the doctor said. "In the thirty-plus years that chemical company's been dumping its waste into Uta-Kaze Bay, it's never admitted that the waste is lethal with mercury. A few token agreements to be legally safe. Are you all right, Sergeant?"

Wood nodded. They went back through the silent corridors to the doctor's office. Wood lit a cigarette.

"The mercury poisoned the fish and shellfish," the doctor said. "That's about all the people eat in Uta-Kaze. Celia Pearson loved fish and shellfish, a craving in her pregnancy, too. She ate the local catch almost every day she was in Uta-Kaze. They hadn't really known about the sickness then; the chemical company had kept it hushed up. Celia escaped with perhaps a tiny damage, the child didn't. Mr. Pearson doesn't like fish much."

"All right, hide it," Wood said. "But murder? Blackmail? Just to hide Sarah Pearson's existence?"

"It would seem extreme, Sergeant."

"Could someone in Japan have known?"

"I don't see how. We certainly never told anyone in or from Japan."

"Were there ever any visitors who could have seen Sarah Pearson, or learned about her from Celia? Before twelve years ago? Has Sarah ever been away from this sanitarium?"

"Never, and no visitors except the Pearsons."

"Cornelius Hook?"

"No, I've never seen him here or heard the Pearsons say he even knows."

Wood shook his head. "Maybe I'm all wrong, barking up a wrong tree. Something else behind the murders."

The doctor said nothing. Murder wasn't his field.

*

Wood had to detour around San Vincente, a highway bridge out over the main creek. In Monteverde they were still holding the Santa Rosa River. In the night, Alice Garnet's apartment was dark. Her car was parked in front. Wood knocked. There was no answer. He looked in at the front windows, saw nothing. He thought for a moment, then got out his ring of keys.

Inside her apartment he listened. He heard nothing. He walked through the small apartment. There were two glasses on the low coffee table in front of the couch, the beginnings of a dinner on the kitchen stove. The pans of soup were cold, the cheese cut on bread but not put into the broiler. Wood went to the closed bedroom door. He opened it.

The bedroom was empty, the bed made and not slept in. The closets were full only of clothes. No suitcases seemed missing. Out in the cluttered living room there were stubs in the ashtray beside the two almost-empty glasses. Wood smelled the glasses. Whisky and nothing more. He did not see Alice Garnet's handbag. The bathroom was clean and empty.

Wood went back to his car, drove away.

*

In the dark at the corner of the next building of the garden apartment, Alice Garnet and James Pearson watched Wood drive off. Alice looked up at the tall executive.

"Donny? Why did we hide?"

"I don't want to talk to Wood. Not now. I don't want his questions, no more of them. I don't want to talk," James Pearson said. "Come back inside, okay?"

They went back to her apartment, went in and locked the door behind them, sat on the couch.

"He's looking for you, Donny," Alice said.

"I know. He's learning all about Celia, about Sarah."

"I never knew it wasn't a miscarriage. How awful for both of you, Donny. You should have told me."

"No, tell no one. Celia would have gone crazy."

Alice picked up her glass. The drink was warm, flat. She got up, went toward the kitchen with both drinks.

"She knew the child was dead," she said. "What else was there to drive her crazy?"

Pearson shook his head violently. "Nothing!"

Alice came back with the fresh drinks. Pearson gulped his like a man in some desert. Alice sipped at hers, didn't sit.

"Wood found no death certificate, Donny," she said.

"He found that?"

"He wonders where the child died. How she died."

"She died! That's all! My Sarah! Nothing I could do to help her, nothing!" He gulped at his whisky. "I did what anyone would have done. We decided, the sensible thing.

I'm not ashamed. It was my life, too, my future."

Pearson drained his glass, looked at it as if his world was somewhere in it. "My life, I have to accept it. I agreed, the only smart way. You can only endure so much, though. Fall apart now. I tried to stop it this time, but—" The violent shake of his head again. "I don't want to talk about it anymore, the past. No more about what's past."

"Donny?" Alice said. "What've you done?"

"Done?" He smiled up at her. "Failed, that's what I did. That's all, just failed."

"You came to me that night," Alice said, wet her lips with her whisky. "The first time in months. Why, Donny? You came here, and you left at midnight. The night Sam was shot. Where did you go? Why come to me that night?"

"Go? To the country club. Where else does a man with a sick wife go?" Pearson said. "She got sick at the airport, Alice. The spell coming, I saw it. So I came to you. Where else have I gone for twenty-two years? You and the club. I told you to leave, go away, get free of me."

"I know you did," Alice said. "Just to the club, Donny? The night Sam was killed?"

"The gloomy drinker, a late supper," Pearson said, nodding as if seeing himself alone in the country club. He looked up again, his face suddenly boyish, his eyes clear. "Still time, honey? Why not? You and me, we'll both go away. Let it all fall apart, we'll start over. Maybe that's why I came to you that night, you see? I knew it had to all go, begin again, what I always should have done. No more protecting. Myself!"

"Us?" Alice said.

Pearson reached up, held her, pulled her down on the couch beside him. He kissed her like a boy with a new girl. Her free hand went up to the back of his head, held him.

"You'd have to talk to Sergeant Wood sometime, Donny," Alice said. "Can you talk to him?"

"Wood? Yes, of course. That would have to be done first. If I just knew—?" Pearson laughed. "By God we can, Alice! A life, all new, somewhere else. Why not?"

"Celia?" she said. "Wood went back to L.A. About the death certificate."

"Back?" Pearson's face clouded. "Then he'll find . . . But that's all right. If only—?" His eyes were far away. "Alice, would Sam have had a secret apartment? A house? For women, perhaps, special?"

"I don't think so, Donny. The house he spent so much money on, the boat, the old lodge. That's all I—"

"Lodge?" Pearson stood up, knocked over his empty glass. "The old lodge!"

He strode out, leaving the door open. Alice Garnet stared after him.

*

Below the hill of Cornelius Hook's house Vaal Creek was over its banks, flooding the lower terraces. Wood hurried through the rain. Old Hook opened the door before he got there.

"Leave your slicker in the entry, Sergeant," Hook said.

Wood hung his slicker, went into the study. Alan Pearson and Jitsuko Ikeda were there.

"Have you seen Pearson?" Wood asked.

"Not since this afternoon," old Hook said.

Alan and Jitsuko shook their heads.

"He's not at his house, no one is, all dark. He's not at the country club or at his office. They need him at the plant, the river's still rising, and they don't know where he is," Wood said. "I've been back to the sanitarium, Mr. Hook."

"Have you?"

"I found her, Sarah. I know. But—"

Alan Pearson said, "Found her? *Found?* Then she's alive? My sister? Grandfather, all this time you never told me?"

Wood told him. Cornelius Hook stood impassive. Alan listened. He turned to a wall, rigid. Jitsuko Ikeda blinked as Wood told about Sarah Pearson and Uta-Kaze, covered her mouth. The room was silent, only the angry rush of Vaal Creek below.

"I'm not sure that was necessary, Sergeant," Hook said.

"Neither am I, but I've got a job," Wood said. "Any one of you could have killed Sam Garnet and Roberta Dunn. It all turns around Yukio Ikeda coming here twelve years ago with some money scheme. Blackmail, it sounds to me. But what happened to Sarah isn't enough. I'm sure of that. Something more."

"Perhaps you're wrong altogether," old Hook said. "Have you seen Alice Garnet since you came back this time?"

"No, why?"

"A thought," Hook said blandly.

Wood studied the old man. "You had George Thesiger beaten?"

"You're asking me, Sergeant? You want a confession?"

"You're the silent power behind River Enterprises, behind Sam Garnet. Thesiger didn't know that, wanted to take over."

"George has changed his mind. He's on my side now. He'll join the company," Hook said. He thought. "Still,

George *did* want to operate River Enterprises very much. Anne always pushing him, eh? I'm afraid that he thought that with Sam Garnet gone, all he had to do was persuade Alice Garnet. He didn't know that there were other, ah, factors."

"You're accusing Thesiger of killing Sam Garnet?"

"Not at all," Hook said. "But with poor Sarah hardly a strong enough motive, it does open another avenue."

"How about Vinnie Tugela? Maybe he wanted to go up in the world. Thought that if Garnet was out of the way, he could side with you against Thesiger and get rewarded."

"It's a possibility," Hook agreed. "An ambitious young man."

Wood said, "If you see Jim Pearson, hold him and call us. All of you understand that?"

Alan and Jitsuko nodded. Cornelius Hook sat down, patted his pockets for a cigar.

19

In the night, the Thesiger house gushed from all its downspouts. A white-uniformed nurse let Wood in.

George Thesiger lay on the couch in the living room. His arm was in a cast and sling. His whole head and jaw were bandaged, and his nose was raw and swollen. Both eyes were puffed a livid yellow-black. Anne Thesiger sat near him. She had a dark-colored drink.

"I thought a week in the hospital?" Wood said.

Anne Thesiger said, "He wanted to come home. They said he could if we had a nurse. Have you arrested Tugela, my father?"

"Will your husband testify against them?"

On the couch George Thesiger wasn't looking at Wood. His jaw was wired, and his eyes were fixed up at space.

"I don't know," Anne said. "He wants to take the vice-presidency at Hook Instrument, sell River. I'm damned if I do now!"

"You'd fight your father?"

"If I could just—!" Anne shuddered. "Wait until George can talk. Did you check on Sam Garnet and my sister?"

"Garnet couldn't have been the father of the baby back

in Japan," Wood said. "But you were right about one thing, there wasn't any miscarriage."

He told them all he had learned in Los Angeles. George Thesiger turned toward Wood slowly, his blackened eyes wide. Anne Thesiger was gray.

"Something worse than a miscarriage," Wood said. Something to hide, to drive your sister half crazy. But murder?"

Anne Thesiger nodded, seemed to have no words to say. A childless woman, but feeling the horror of Sarah Pearson.

"If Yukio Ikeda had something to sell, what was it?" Wood said. "Just that Sarah Pearson existed? It's not enough."

"A stain on the family?" Anne Thesiger said.

Wood said, "Your father? Revenge, Mrs. Thesiger?"

"No," she said, shook her head. "Not even him."

"Where was your father in March, 1962?"

"Here, I suppose. I remember he complained that Jim Pearson was away from the office taking care of Alan while Celia and we were in Palm Springs. But he couldn't have—"

"Anyway," Wood said, "if just knowing about Sarah was Yukio Ikeda's blackmail, how did he find out? He was about eight when Sarah was born. He never left Sakai in Japan."

"How could he have known?" Anne agreed.

"Unless Sarah alone wasn't the blackmail," Wood said. "Say some other man *was* the father. Some man here, not in Japan. She was pregnant when she went over. Say Yukio Ikeda came to blackmail that real father twelve years ago."

George Thesiger was watching Wood now.

"Say that real father and Sam Garnet got rid of Yukio Ikeda. Now Jitsuko shows up. Sam Garnet decides to take care of her before she can cause trouble, even accidentally. The real father meets Sam at the motel—but then he sees something better, his chance. So he kills Garnet, tries to take over River."

Anne Thesiger said, "Are you serious, Sergeant?"

"I'm serious," Wood said, looked at Thesiger.

The beaten man was waving his good arm, pointing at a pad and pencil. Anne Thesiger gave them to him. He wrote

"Wouldn't the real father have wanted the Ikeda girl out of the way first, if your theory is right?" Anne said.

"Say he wasn't as scared of her as Garnet, the chance was better," Wood said. "Or it could be his wife helped him out."

George Thesiger waved the pad at Wood. Anne took it, gave it to Wood. Thesiger had written: *It's a damned lie! I never went near Sam Garnet!*

"Were you Celia Pearson's lover back then?" Wood said.

"No he wasn't!" Anne said. "And be careful about accusing me of anything, Wood."

Thesiger waved for the pad again, wrote furiously, tossed it at Wood. Wood picked it up, read it: *I don't chase skirts in back streets! I'm not Jim Pearson. Maybe that's what your Ikeda knew!*

All at once Wood's throat was dry.

"What woman did Jim Pearson chase, Thesiger?"

"Jim Pearson?" Anne said. "He has a woman?"

Thesiger waved for the pad. Wood took it to him. Thesiger wrote. Wood didn't want to look at it. He knew, it slid into place like an oiled gear. Donny. Wood looked at the pad: *Alice Garnet, didn't you know? Since she was seventeen. Real careful, never seen together, but Sam knew.*

Anne Thesiger read the note. "All these years, and you never told me? A weapon like that? You could have had any job in the company! Your own company! My father would have given anything to hide it from Celia! From the town! You fool! Look at you! Beaten up, a flunky! Too late, you damned fool!"

George Thesiger turned toward the back of the couch, his face hidden. Anne Thesiger's face was sick. For the lost opportunity, for Thesiger, mostly for herself.

Wood saw and heard none of it. He saw the small clue he had missed. Sarah Pearson's birth certificate—Father: James *Donald* Pearson. Donny. Since Alice Garnet was seventeen—and maybe not over yet.

*

The rain poured down on the headquarters parking lot, and Wood sat there in his car. He didn't get out, go in to his desk. He had a job, but he sat in his car.

Had she lied? Not by commission, he hadn't asked, but by omission? As a man? What right did he have to know, to judge? Unless it was still going on. Even then . . . ?

As a cop? If it was still going on? He should have known, as a cop. Important information, even a motive. Where was she now? Where was James Pearson?

Wood got out of his car, went inside to his desk in the squad room. Phil Martin spoke to him as he passed. Wood didn't answer. At his desk he picked up his telephone, dialed Alice Garnet's number. It rang four times. He started to hang up.

"Yes?" Her voice at the other end.

Wood hung up. She was home. Alone? It wasn't something he could find out over the telephone, or do. He got up.

"Sergeant?" It was the duty sergeant at his desk. "You got another visitor. You're collecting Japs. A girl."

Jitsuko Ikeda came into the squad room. She walked with her head up, but her dark eyes flitted around at all the policemen in the busy room. Wood sat down, nodded her to a chair. She wore her Chinese dress, held a small handbag.

"You want to see me, Jitsuko?" Wood said. He felt tired.

"Yes. I have lied to you, Sergeant Wood. I did not come here as a friend. I came for hate, and for money."

"Blackmail? On what?"

She nodded. "In Japan I hated America. Yukio did not come back from America. At Tanaka I learned how rich Mr. Pearson and Mr. Garnet were. I came to make them pay me for silence." She hesitated. "But now . . . Alan has been so nice, so kind. When I have been lying with smiles. I . . . I like him, Sergeant."

"To blackmail James Pearson, too?" Wood said. "What made you think Pearson had anything to do with Yukio? That letter only mentioned Sam Garnet."

"There was another letter." She opened her handbag. "It was written earlier. From Los Angeles."

The letter was postmarked on March 15, 1962.

"Read it to me," Wood said.

"Honorable Uncle," Jitsuko read. *"I have left my ship. Do not worry, I am going to make much money in America. There are people named Pearson and Garnet who will pay much money for what I have. I have prepared well. Respect, Yukio."*

Wood took the letter. He looked at the Japanese characters as if they would tell him the answers.

"Pearson and Garnet. That's all? No first names?"

"That is all," Jitsuko said.

"Something he *had*," Wood said. "That doesn't have to be blackmail." He put the letter aside. "Why tell me now?"

"Tonight, when you told us of that girl—" She clenched her small hands. "In Japan I was so clever, so sure I would come and fool the rich Americans. So pleased, a daring venture on a faraway stage. But here, now—?"

She touched her tiny fists to Wood's desk. "Here it is *real*. Real sorrow, real pain, real murder! I had a fairy tale of revenge for poor Yukio! But Yukio was not doing a good thing, we knew that. My uncle never dared to show the letters. And I came to do something not good. But real people are hurt. Real people bleed, are . . . dead. Tonight, when you told of Sarah Pearson, it was real. Terrible. The men in Japan who did that do not feel the real pain, yes? Am I like them?"

Her eyes denied it. "Somewhere there is a real murderer. Who will be . . . I had to come to you, tell you. Alan is hurt, unhappy. Because of me. I hope, perhaps, we can try again."

"Yeh," Wood said. "Is that all of it, Jitsuko? Sure?"

"I am sure."

"Okay," Wood said.

When Jitsuko had gone, Wood looked at the letter again. Its Japanese seemed to mock him. He got his slicker.

*

Alice Garnet walked back into her apartment. Wood saw the unmade bed through her open bedroom door. Earlier, it had been made. Alice lit a cigarette, turned to him, saw his face.

"So you know?"

"Why not tell me?" Wood said. "James *Donald* Pearson.

Did you always call him Donny, or was that for my benefit?"

"I always called him that. Seventeen at the start."

"All right, you had no reason to tell Wood the man. But Sergeant Wood the cop? What about Yukio Ikeda? You were Pearson's girl twelve years ago, too."

"I didn't know anything about Yukio Ikeda. Donny didn't—"

Wood told her about the second letter: Pearson and Garnet.

"No first names," Wood said. "What Pearson, what Garnet?"

She shook her head. "No one knew about us, Harry."

"Thesiger did, and Sam. Maybe Ikeda did, too."

"Donny wouldn't—" She looked for an ashtray. "He was here with me the night Sam was shot. The first time in months. He left at midnight. I never thought . . . He was at the club."

"Yeh, but no one saw him there after about one-fifteen," Wood said. "What do you think now, Alice?"

"I don't know, Harry." She didn't look behind her to the bedroom. "He was here tonight. Worried. About Celia, he said."

"Who are you worried about?"

She sat down. "He was so alone back then, Harry. Celia was always sick, never with him. Just when he was working so hard to build Hook Instrument, needed a woman. I fell in love. No strings. We had wonderful times. He's a gentle man, I was his hiding place. He always went back to Celia, had Alan, and I slowly realized he'd never leave her. She was part of his life and work, a major part. Too many complications to break."

"You still love him?"

"I don't know." She stubbed out her cigarette.

"Where did he go from here, Alice?"

"He talked about Sam's old lodge. In the mountains. I'm not sure anyone could reach it in this flooding."

Wood went to the door. Alice got her coat. Wood stopped, tried to see behind her eyes. He couldn't. They went out.

20

The county highway crossed the upper Santa Rosa River on a steel bridge fifteen miles from Monteverde. A blacktop road went on up into the mountains. The rain blinded Wood's windshield, and the blacktop turned into dirt as the road climbed. Wood fought the steering wheel as the car slid and yawed across creeks and among the dark trees.

"There!" Alice shouted above the rain.

Wood saw a lake below in a steep valley. He saw the shape of a rambling pine lodge. They parked, got out in the rain. A high, deep creek ran into the lake between the road and the lodge. Another branch of the creek ran into the lake behind the lodge that stood on an island of land between the two creeks and the lake. A footbridge crossed the near creek to the lodge.

Wood helped Alice across the narrow bridge to the lodge. The front door was locked.

"A nail under the steps!" Alice said in the windy rain.

Wood found the nail. There was no key.

"Try the back!" Alice said.

They went around the lodge. The back door was swinging open, blowing in the rain. Wood pushed Alice behind him, went inside first. He clicked the light switch. It worked.

"Harry!"

The lodge had been searched. A violent search, frantic. Rugs were up, drawers out, tables overturned. But an incomplete search, the big main room only two-thirds chaos, some cabinets and a bureau untouched as if the mess had been cut with a knife. Wood took out his pistol.

"Come on out!" he called.

There was only silence, and the rain, and then the car motor started up somewhere in the distance across the creek. Wood ran to the front windows. The car motor faded away along the road back toward the county highway. Wood saw nothing.

"He must have heard us, had a car hidden off the road."

"Donny? I mean, Jim Pearson?"

"Probably," Wood said. "But I don't think he got what he wanted. We interrupted him."

Wood began to search the rustic lodge. He ignored what had been searched, began where the mess ended. Alice Garnet sat in a heavy wooden chair and watched him. The lodge was cold, she pulled her coat around her, her legs tucked up under it. Wood worked through the big main room, and on into the bedrooms. Alice smoked. The rumble of the creeks shook the lodge. It took an hour. Then Wood came out of an inner bedroom. He held a long sheet of lined paper with writing filling it.

"In a bedroom closet, under a floorboard," Wood said. "An old hiding place. Other things, too—stocks, Sam's first contract as security chief for Hook Instrument, an old address book with names I recognize. Underworld names, fixers, mostly down in L.A." He read the paper in his hand. "But I think this is what our searcher wanted."

"What is it, Harry?"

"A page from the register of The Rosa Hotel for March, 1962. It shows that Yukio Ikeda checked in on March 15, 1962, all right. But it doesn't show any checkout for Ikeda. Other people on the page checked in after March 15 and checked out after March 22, but Ikeda didn't check out."

Wood put the page aside. "This has to be what Sam's house was searched for the murder night. It must have been taken out of the register twelve years ago, and a fake page substituted so our detective would think Ikeda had checked out. The two witnesses who 'saw' Ikeda board the Frisco bus must have been paid."

"Couldn't someone have just filled in the real page?"

"The handwriting wouldn't have matched. Ikeda signed in, he had a particular handwriting. Our detective would have seen the difference if the whole page hadn't been forged."

"Sam kept the real page?"

"A weapon against someone."

"Then Ikeda must . . . he must have been—"

"He didn't check out, that's all. There could be more than one reason why that would be hidden. I—"

The sound seemed to rise out of the night itself. A massive rumbling like the growl of some giant animal. The lodge shook, and out in the night a noise of tearing mixed with the rumble.

"What? Harry?" Alice cried.

Wood ran to the front door. Fifty feet up the creek the water seemed to rise ten feet higher. A wall of water above the normal surface, flashing white with torn tree trunks and boulders carried like pebbles.

"A crest!" Wood shouted. "Something gave way upstream!"

The mass of water, trees and boulders roared past and on out into the lake, boiling the surface as it spread. Water spread almost to the lodge, and seethed out in the lake for a few long minutes before it slowly subsided.

The rainy night seemed almost silent.

"Alice," Wood said.

The footbridge across the flooded creek was gone.

*

Wood came back into the lodge. Alice had found food, was making some dinner on an electric stove. The lights still worked. Wood had been out in the night for almost an hour.

"No way out tonight," he said. "I guess we're marooned."

"You're cold and wet. Eat something. It's hash."

Wood hung up his slicker, stood warming for a few minutes at the fire in a mammoth fireplace. She had built the fire, too, while he was out in the rain, cordwood stacked beside the fireplace. Quite a woman, her copper hair loose again, and reflecting the firelight.

"Come while it's hot, Harry," she said, held his chair out.

She had found a man's heavy cardigan, wore it like a starlet in an old movie who came out of the man's bedroom wearing only his pajama top. The teen-age boy's dream—marooned in a mountain lodge with a girl in a pajama top. Wood didn't laugh, he suddenly felt too hollow down in his belly.

There were peas to go with the hash, and coffee not too stale. Wood ate all there was, hungrier than he had realized. She ate little, lit a cigarette with her coffee, counted the cigarettes left in her pack.

"I've got a full pack, almost," Wood said, pushed his plate away, and grinned at her now. "We'll make it through the night."

She smiled. "I expect we will."

He poured a fresh cup of the coffee for himself, sat back. He listened to the rain for a time, the steady surge of the two creeks. The rain seemed to be a little less heavy. Alice smoked, drank her coffee, traced a pattern with her finger on the table.

"Harry?" she said. "You think it was Jim Pearson here after that register page?"

"I'm not sure, Alice."

"You think he killed Sam, probably Yukio Ikeda years ago?"

"He could be protecting someone else."

"But you think Yukio Ikeda was murdered, Sam was involved with someone else, and that's why Sam was murdered?"

"Maybe." Wood sipped his coffee. "Only if Sam and someone else got rid of Yukio Ikeda twelve years ago, and Sam was afraid of Jitsuko, wouldn't the someone else be just as scared of her? Why murder Sam instead of Jitsuko? Unless the other person was more afraid of Sam and that register page, took his chance to be free of Sam, end it."

"End it?" Alice said. "Harry, it has to be Donny—Jim Pearson—or one of us here. That's what you think?"

"It could still have been someone else, an outsider. From Sam's police days, or some shady deal. Someone could have followed him up from L.A."

"No, you don't think that. One of us here in Monteverde." She picked up her cup, found it empty, poured more coffee. She stirred the coffee even though it was black. "Harry, who will it all help? Is Sam worth any more suffering? You say he was going to murder Jitsuko Ikeda, he was probably a blackmailer. Yukio Ikeda was a blackmailer, or worse."

"Roberta Dunn?" Wood said.

"Who knows for sure what she was doing?" She went on stirring the coffee that didn't need it. "Harry, old Hook has offered to buy my shares of River Enterprises for more than they're worth. Enough money to finally get out of Monteverde. Go somewhere, have a better life. Really paint, maybe."

"*More* than they're worth? Why?"

"So I'll take you away with me." She finally drank her coffee, looked at Wood. "He'll give you money, too. A lot of money, I expect."

She waited, but Wood was silent.

"He has the money," she said. "He wants his family free of the trouble. Sarah hidden, I suppose, nothing exposed. He wants the case unsolved, closed."

"Do you, Alice?"

She sat back in her chair. "I'm not sure I care one way or the other. About Yukio Ikeda, or about who killed Sam. I guess I'm not much better than Sam was. My father believed in all our success myths, and when they failed him, he didn't hate the myths, just his failure. The system wasn't a failure, *he* was, or there was a conspiracy against him. Both."

She lit another cigarette. "When you grow up seeing that, there're only two ways to go—become amoral, take every advantage of the phony myths, win over other people; or drop out and oppose. Sam took the amoral way, self-interest only, get his. I suppose I did, too. In a smaller way. Half-assed."

"There's a third way," Wood said. "Try to make it all work, do your own job."

"Does it work? Will they let you, give you any respect or a share? Or is that my father, end with nothing and bitter?"

Wood finished his coffee, reached for his cigarettes. He lit one. He smoked, and the rain beat on the lodge roof.

"How much money is Hook offering?" he said.

"You'd be comfortable, I expect."

"Away from here."

"He didn't say that, but I'd like to go. New York, Europe, the whole world. A lot better life."

"With me?"

Her eyes had that wide, all-surface look of a woman waiting in bed. "If you want me, Harry, yes."

"Donny? Is that all over?"

"He'll never leave Celia," she said. She frowned, not what she had meant to say. "Before I met you, I wasn't sure. I had nothing else. I told myself it was over, we hadn't been seeing each other that much, but I didn't know for sure. I guess I didn't want to know. But now I've got something else."

"Would you marry me?"

"Yes."

Wood went around the table to her. She looked up at him. He took out his pistol, looked at it for a moment. Then he put it on the table. He took Alice's hand, and they walked into one of the two bedrooms.

*

The sun woke Wood, and a kind of silence. The silence of no rain, and the clear whistles of birds. Alice lay asleep in the bed beside him. Wood lit a cigarette, sat up against the wall behind the bed. Everything was sun and the birds outside, but Wood didn't smile as he smoked.

The bedroom, and the creeks running outside, made Wood think of his own house. A small, cheap cottage. A cop's salary. A cop fourteen years in a flat, dusty city that could blow away and no one would miss it much. Owned by the Hooks and Sam Garnets, served by the Thesigers and Vinnie Tugelas.

Wood got up, opened a window, breathed the mountain air of a sunny morning. Across the muddy slope behind the lodge, the creek branched and flowed into the lake, the streams lower now. The crest wave last night had collapsed a section of the bank on the lodge side. Wood stared out, turned quickly, and began to dress.

He carried a shovel from the toolroom when he crossed the muddy slope to where the bank had washed away. The skeleton lay exposed where it had been buried in the bank some five feet down. Wood climbed down, saw the crushed break in the skull on the left side. A small skeleton, and of a young man. Wood kneeled down.

There were rotted traces of some heavy denim cloth like sailors' pants. A decayed wallet with nothing recognizable in it. A metal key ring and some coins. And a hotel key caked with mud. The coins were Japanese. A medallion on the key ring read: Tanaka Instruments, Sakai, Japan. The hotel key was from the Rosa Hotel.

Alice Garnet, dressed, stood above Wood in the exposed hole on the creek bank.

"Yukio Ikeda," Wood said.

He climbed up and began to walk along the stream. Alice followed him as he searched the lowered creek for a way across.

"Harry," Alice said. "Last night? We—"

"I have to know all there is," Wood said. "We'll talk again later."

Alice nodded. It took Wood almost an hour to find a boulder that jutted out into the creek with a tree lodged against it and debris piled against the tree. The space between the debris and the far bank was less than five feet.

They got their things, and Wood walked out onto the tree. It was solid enough. Wood jumped to the far bank. He held his hand out for Alice. She fell a foot short, but Wood caught her and pulled her up.

21

The sandbag levee had held the Santa Rosa River, the imminent flood danger over in Monteverde. Wood took Alice Garnet home before he drove to headquarters. There were no messages at his desk. He ordered an APB on James Pearson, and went out again.

The old farmhouse up the barranca was deserted, Tugela's red Impala not there. Wood drove south on the freeway to Cuyama Beach. Debris littered the highway, and two creeks were over their banks in Fremont. It was almost lunchtime before Wood parked at the marina in Cuyama Beach.

Vinnie Tugela worked in the cockpit of the *Sea King II*. The sea was down, the sun bright. Tugela worked in his shirtsleeves, his muscles alive.

"Hook gave you the boat?" Wood asked.

"River Enterprises did, a grateful company," Tugela said.

"You're all set. Unless George Thesiger talks."

"About what, Sergeant?" Tugela said. "His word against mine. What proof? Besides, he won't talk."

"I guess not," Wood said. "But it won't help you much."

Tugela stopped working, looked up at Wood on the

dock. Wood took out the old register page from The Rosa Hotel.

"I found Yukio Ikeda. Buried twelve years ago, his head bashed in." Wood held the register page. "This page proves you covered a murder. That's a felony. You better tell me now."

Tugela stood up, sat against the gunwale.

"You were night clerk at The Rosa then," Wood said.

Tugela licked at his lips. "Sam Garnet sent Ikeda to The Rosa. Garnet was a big cop then, I owed him. He told me to keep an eye on Ikeda, his phone calls, anyone he met."

"What was Ikeda doing in Monteverde?"

"Sam never said. Just watch the Jap kid. Ikeda never did get any calls or meet anyone. Then Sam had me drive Ikeda up to meet him at the Pearson place. Sam was romancing Roberta Dunn up there. Sam and Ikeda talked. They set up a meeting in the Jap's room at The Rosa. Something went wrong, Ikeda got killed."

"So you buried him at Garnet's lodge?"

"Not me! I helped Sam carry the body out of the hotel, that's all. Two days later we remembered the register. Someone might come looking. So we put in that faked page, had two guys say they saw the Jap get on the Frisco bus. It worked. Cops came once, then it was all okay."

"Until Jitsuko Ikeda showed up with Alan Pearson."

"Yeh," Tugela said. "I was in deep enough, and Sam Garnet had kept that register page. I wrote up the faked page back then, I had to go along with Garnet now. Then he got killed!"

"Jitsuko Ikeda didn't know about you. Sam Garnet was more danger than she was. That why you killed Garnet?"

"I didn't! I told you how it happened. I found him dead."

"You searched Garnet's house? For this page?"

"Not me. I knew Sam didn't have it there. I stayed away."

"So Garnet killed Yukio Ikeda?"

Tugela shook his head. "Sam was down at the desk with me when it happened up in Ikeda's room. Someone else was up there."

"Who? Who met with Yukio Ikeda?"

"I never saw. Whoever it was called down. Sam went up and got whoever it was out before he called me up to help."

"And you don't know what it was all about?"

"Only something that happened in Japan," Tugela said. "That Ikeda got drunk one day, said something funny—bloodwater pays blood money, he said. He laughed about it."

"But Sam Garnet knew who killed Ikeda, and why?"

"I guess so," Tugela said.

"Maybe you'll remember more in the cell. Climb up."

Tugela climbed off the boat. They went to Wood's car.

*

Vinnie Tugela was booked on two counts of failing to report a murder, one of accessory to murder, and Wood drove to the Pearson home. No one answered the door, and the red Jaguar was alone in the garage. He drove to Hook Instrument. Pearson was still missing, and old Hook wasn't there. Wood tried the country club without finding anyone. He drove back downtown to Alice's apartment.

A car drove away from the garden apartments, and a flash of copper-red hair caught Wood's eye. He watched the car move off. It was a rental car with a Los Angeles plate. Wood followed it.

It drove into Brandwater. Wood dropped back in the

open streets of the suburb that had once been Andrew Hoek's farm. If Alice were in the car . . . He tailed it to the old house of Cornelius Hook above Vaal Creek. As he drove past, Alice and James Pearson got out and went into Hook's house.

Wood parked, worked his way back through the late-afternoon shadows of the tall eucalyptus trees. Only the rental car was in the turnaround, and Wood heard voices in Hook's library. Through the closed window, the small library was dim.

Alice Garnet sat in a straight chair in front of a small mahogany desk. She wasn't smoking now. James Pearson paced the room. Wood could hear Pearson's voice, but not what the tall man was saying. Wood tried to see Alice's face, but it was lost in shadow. His stomach felt empty. Were her eyes sad or happy, worried or excited?

There was no one else in the room, and James Pearson had no weapon Wood could see. He went around the house to the side door. It was unlocked. Wood went in and through to the library. Pearson heard him, turned. Wood had his hand on his pistol.

"Sergeant Wood?" Pearson said.

The tall man stopped pacing. Wood kept his hand on his pistol in its side holster.

"He came to my apartment," Alice said. "He's going to leave Monteverde, start over. He wants me to go with him. We came to get some money from Mr. Hook."

"He should be here," Pearson said, looked at his watch. He took a deep breath. "There must still be time for Alice and me. I owe her that, if she'll have an old man. Not too old, and good at my work. I built the Tanaka valve sales, Cornelius only saw the opportunity. He'll buy me out, give us a start."

"I'm sorry," Wood said. "You can't leave yet."

"You mean Celia? No, I did my best. Too much. Cornelius won't like it, but I must try. My own life."

"I mean a murder case, Mr. Pearson," Wood said.

"Murder? But I don't have time to waste!"

Alice said, "I can't go with you, Donny."

"Can't?" Pearson was surprised. "Why not?"

"I don't want to go with you," Alice said.

"But—?" Pearson nodded. "Too late? Yes, I suppose so." He nodded again. "I tried to stop it this time. The gun was there on the desk. I wanted to stop him. Too late, though."

"Desk?" Wood said. "You had to stop Sam Garnet?"

Pearson sighed. "He was going to kill Jitsuko, you see? Another death. I had to shoot him."

They saw it now. Alice looked away, Wood watched James Pearson. An unreal calm about the tall man, vague and detached. As if he were alone in a thick fog on a deserted street. Wood and Alice not there. The reasonable voice a little weary, but unconnected to the reality of the words.

"You have a gun now, Mr. Pearson?" Wood asked.

"Gun? I don't own a gun, Sergeant."

Wood stepped closer, patted Pearson for a weapon. Pearson seemed a little annoyed, nothing more. Wood found no weapon, stepped back. James Pearson sat down.

"Yukio Ikeda, too?" Wood said. "Twelve years ago?"

Pearson sighed again. "I'm not sorry about that. He was going to talk to Celia. I got her away to Palm Springs, but he said he could always find her. He was a slimy boy. I hit him with a bottle. In that room."

"Which side of the head?" Wood said.

"The left, I think. I'm right-handed. I don't think I meant to hit him so hard, more than once, but he couldn't talk to Celia. We buried him at the lodge. He deserved to die, but I couldn't let Sam kill the girl, too."

"Garnet called you? At the club?"

"He wanted me to help him. I went to the motel. He had a plan to kidnap Jitsuko, simulate an accident in a car. He'd called Japan to be sure. I couldn't let it happen again."

"Then you searched his house for the register page?"

"I remembered he still had the page as I drove home. I thought it wise to find it, destroy it. But it wasn't in the house. I tried at the lodge last night, but someone came. Jitsuko almost caught me at Sam's house, too. You know, I think she did come here to blackmail us? The way she had to grow up, I suppose."

He sighed once more, as if his body couldn't get enough air, looked toward Alice without really seeing her.

"Then you went to Roberta Dunn? She knew—"

Pearson still looked at Alice, through her. "Most people's lives, their characters, are determined simply by where they grew up. The time and place. A few by who their parents were, no matter where they grew up. But some lives are made by one moment, you see? One event, a moment of choice. I had my moment and I took a choice. Everything else came after."

"What choice, Mr. Pearson?" Wood said.

Pearson turned as if slapped. "What? No, I'm not ashamed, I don't regret it. It was the only logical step, the way we have to live. It couldn't hurt anyone, and nothing was going to help. Still—" He seemed to lose his thought, searched for it in his mind, through the fog. "I suppose I'd do the same again, a product of our time and place. But it led to so many things I had to do. Things I never wanted. So many times I wanted to just walk away. Well, it's over, now I can."

"We'll both walk," Wood said. "I have to arrest you."

"Arrest?" Pearson considered that, something that hadn't occurred to him. "Of course, I'm sorry."

He stood up, began to wander around the small library like a large animal in a small cage. He looked along the shelves of books as if he urgently needed something to read.

"Harry?" Alice said. "He's sick."

"Too sick. I've got to take him in." Wood watched the tall man wander around the library. "I guess I won't be rich."

Pearson began to talk again, over his shoulder as he moved aimlessly, looking at no one. "After I killed Ikeda, that seemed to have settled it, you see? No more trouble for so long, a few brief minor spells. I was so sure it was over. Then Alan brought the girl. I couldn't let Sam—"

He stopped moving, touched a row of tall books. "I suppose I'm a naive man, an innocent. I listened to what they told me was the only thing to do. Sam said there was only one way to deal with blackmailers. I listened to Cornelius, too. You give your consent to their ways, and then you can't do anything else. They own you, in their hands."

He turned, his face suddenly puzzled. "What went wrong? How? I only did what any man would do, should do. We all have to have ambition, seize our chance. It hurt no one, did no more harm. Then . . . well, the rest was simple necessity, you see?" He frowned, listened to himself. "One immoral step, and the second and third are inevitable. You go on."

He looked at the tall books, touched one. "Do you know

Krishnamurti, Sergeant? An intelligent man. He wrote that ambition is always destructive, immoral."

The tall man took out a book, seemed to stroke it as if it were alive. He stood there like a brooding statue.

"We better go now, Mr. Pearson," Wood said.

When Pearson put the book back, he knocked the whole row of books over. Nervous and apologetic, he steadied the row with both hands, and when he turned to Wood he had a pistol.

"I'm sorry," he said. "I really can't go with you."

The pistol in Pearson's hand was a 1914 Japanese army Nambu, 8-mm. Wood didn't move. Alice jumped up.

"Donny!"

"No!" Wood said. "Stand still, Alice!"

The pistol was cocked, the safety off.

"I have to get started, you see?" Pearson said, his voice clear and crisp. "I've waited much too long."

"Mr. Pearson," Wood said, "we'll just go down to—"

"I wish I had time," Pearson said. He glanced around the small room. "That closet over there. Please?"

Wood walked to the closet, opened it.

"Harry—" Alice said.

"Do what he says, Alice," Wood said.

"Alice?" Pearson said. "Why, we're together, of course. Twenty years. I don't have to protect Celia anymore. Her father can do that now. He owns us all."

Pearson waved the Nambu. Wood stepped into the closet, closed the door. The key turned in the lock. Footsteps walked away.

22

Inside the dark closet Wood drew his pistol. He didn't try the door. Somewhere out in the big house he heard voices. He listened. The voices moved off slowly. The outside door closed. Wood still waited.

The silence of the big house outside the dark closet seemed to stretch. Maybe five minutes.

A car motor started out in front, the car faded away.

Wood holstered his pistol, braced against the closet walls, began to kick at the door. A heavy door that didn't give an inch. Wood examined the lock in the dim light, looked around for something to use to break the door open.

Footsteps came into the library outside. Quick steps. Wood grabbed his gun again, stood as far to his left as he could, fixed his eyes on where the door would open. The key turned in the lock.

"Harry!" Alice said. "He's gone."

Wood stepped from the closet with his pistol alert.

"He talked about where we would go, what we would do," Alice said, "but when we got outside . . . I don't know, he changed. Like that. Out there, in the light, he seemed all of a sudden rational. He *made* me come back."

"Where did he say he was going?"

"Texas, a valve company he knows. He—"

"No," Wood said. "I mean now. Where is he going now?"

She shook her head. "I don't know. He seemed so calm again, his old self."

"That could be worse," Wood said. "Going in and out. He might even have forgotten it all by now. Come on."

Wood hurried her up the quiet Brandwater street to where he had left his car. They drove the short mile to the Pearson house. It was still silent and deserted, the housekeeper still away, Alan and Jitsuko gone somewhere. Wood checked the garage and the cottage. The cottage was empty, and the red Jaguar was still the only car in the garage.

"Where would he go, Harry?" Alice said.

"Anywhere, it depends on what he's thinking," Wood said. "The airport. Drive to L.A. Drive north or east. Maybe to the sanitarium if he's forgotten everything. We better find him, and soon."

He drove downtown to headquarters. He took Alice in with him, and reported it all to Captain Vause.

"Pearson killed them all? Yukio Ikeda, too?" Vause said.

"That's what he told us," Wood said.

"Did he tell you why?"

"Not all of it, talked in circles."

"Then we better find him," Vause said.

They got out calls to all patrol cars near the airport, the bus depot, the train station.

"No train for two hours, though," Vause said.

"Plenty of planes and buses," Wood said.

Vause radioed orders to block the highways out, got in

touch with the Highway Patrol and the Sheriff's office. He alerted every police cruiser out on the streets of the city. It took two hours, and it was dark when they had finished.

Pearson hadn't been seen at the airport, the bus depot, the train station, or on any highway.

"He either got out before we closed it off," Vause said, "or he's still in the city. If he's out, it's going to be up to the other departments to stop him. If he's still inside, we can't cover everywhere. We'll cruise everywhere we know he might go, hound him, and watch."

"He might forget, go about his business normally," Wood said. "I better find the others. Alice better stay here for the night, she could be in danger."

"No," she said, "not from Donny."

"You can't be sure he *is* Donny now," Wood said.

He left her with Vause, went out and drove back to Brandwater. The Pearson house was dark, no gray car near it. Wood tried Sam Garnet's house, and the Thesiger house. Both were dark. He went on to Cornelius Hook's old house. There was light, and two cars stood in the turnaround. One was the white Porsche, the other was Hook's big Cadillac.

*

In the glass-walled study of Hook's house, Wood finished the story. Alan Pearson sat with his thin face turned down to the floor, his hands twisted together. Jitsuko's pale-china face showed little, but her eyes flickered like a moth trapped in a light-shade. James Pearson had killed her brother, but Yukio had come to blackmail, and the others were dead because she had come like her brother.

"You knew about it, Mr. Hook? About Ikeda, too?" Wood said.

The heavy old man stood at his wall of glass like a man

who knows that the view will never be exactly the same again. He turned to look at the poker table, at the chairs that would be empty when the regular game began again.

"No, I didn't know," Hook said. "But it's not a surprise, either. Someone in the family, or close to us. It had to be, didn't it? I should have acted sooner, Sergeant."

"We'll never know," Wood said. "Pearson wouldn't let us."

Hook sat down, a heavy man. "I knew something had happened twelve years ago. I didn't know what, and didn't ask. It all seemed settled. Twelve years with no serious troubles."

"Pearson never told you about Ikeda?" Wood said. "Or Sam Garnet? You worked closely with Garnet."

"They didn't tell me," Hook said.

Alan Pearson looked up at Wood. His eyes showed that he had listened to nothing being said, wrapped up in the concentration of his own thoughts.

"If they both killed Yukio Ikeda, why would my father want to kill Sam Garnet?" he said.

"To stop Garnet from hurting Jitsuko," Wood said. "No more killing. That's what he said. I think he was afraid of Garnet, too, afraid of the past, and of getting in deeper."

Old Hook slapped his thigh hard. "Soft! Underneath, he always was. Broken up because the girl came here. Already irrational."

"You mean he was irrational to try to stop Sam Garnet?" Wood said.

Alan said, "It would have been rational to let Garnet go and kill Suko, Grandfather?"

"More so, yes!" the old man snapped. "She came to blackmail like her brother before her!"

Jitsuko's face was frozen. "I was wrong. I used Alan, tried to. I will go. I am so sorry, Alan."

Alan shook his head. "I don't know, Suko."

"Stupid!" old Hook said, got up again, walked around the warm study on his thick legs. "I should have seen it, not acting like himself. Paralyzed, in a fog."

"Didn't you see it, Mr. Hook?" Wood said.

"I saw trouble in my family, that was all."

"But it's clear now," Wood said. "You're sure Pearson did it all, satisfied."

Both Alan and Jitsuko turned to Wood. Old Hook stopped his ponderous walking around the room.

"Aren't you, Sergeant?" Hook said.

"I'm not sure," Wood said. "He confessed, sounded like he meant it, knew how it happened. But he's detached, playing out a kind of dream, a sense of doom. He's vague, maybe protecting someone."

"Who would my father want to protect?" Alan said.

"You have someone in mind, Sergeant?" old Hook said.

"You tell me, Mr. Hook."

"If you mean Celia, you're wrong," Hook said.

Wood thought. "Not sure who I mean. Pearson knew how Ikeda was killed, and where. He could have known all that by just burying Ikeda, though. I can't pin down *why* he killed Ikeda twelve years ago."

"An accident, you said it yourself," Hook said. "A moment of anger."

"Sure, but I mean the motive. What was Yukio Ikeda's blackmail? What could Ikeda know back then that Mrs. Pearson didn't?"

Hook sat down once more. "Jim didn't say?"

"Not really," Wood said. "He talked about a choice he

made. Any of you know what that could have been?"

None of them answered him. Wood began to button the slicker he still wore from last night and the lodge. Alan Pearson watched him button the raincoat the way Wood had seen witnesses watch the state executioner prepare the gas chamber.

"Have you ever seen a bird trapped in a house?" the thin boy said. "Frantic, flying crazily into walls and windows, desperate to get out?" Alan looked away. "He's my father."

"I know," Wood said. "Only a bird like that can peck your eyes out when you try to help. Panic. If he comes to any of you, try to keep him close, but don't let him too close. Call us. For his sake, too. And it might be a good idea if you all stayed together."

"Alan and the girl can stay here," Hook said.

Wood finished buttoning his slicker.

23

There was no news of Pearson in the squad room. Alice Garnet drank coffee in a corner. She looked very alone.

"We'll do our best to get him unhurt," Wood said.

"Will he hurt anyone else?"

"I hope not. But he's got the gun."

She drank. "What made him change so suddenly? In the library? He seemed to be beaten, doomed, and then—?"

"Something I said. Or maybe he just saw the gun behind those books," Wood said. "Alice, do you know what he was talking about? The choice he made that determined his life?"

"No, Harry, I don't."

"You better try to sleep. If a cell doesn't bother you."

"That's where he'll be the rest of his life, won't he?"

"Something like that," Wood said.

He went out to his car again, made the rounds of all the houses. They were all still dark except Hook's house. Wood drove on to the Hook Instrument plant. Only a watchman was there. Wood told the watchman about Pearson, instructed him to be alert, Pearson might try to hide in the plant.

Then he sat for a time in his car, and had a cigarette. Patrol cars would cruise past all the houses and the plant, check the country club and even Sam Garnet's boat at Cuyama Beach. It was the best a small department could do, and Pearson would expect them to watch all the places associated with him—if he was still rational at all. Then where . . . ?

Wood thought of the lodge.

He drove out of the city, and on into the mountains. The side road to the lodge was better, the creeks down as quickly as they had come up in the heavy rains. The bridge over the creek at the lodge was still out. Wood saw no car and no light, but he crossed the creek anyway. There was no one in the lodge.

On his way back to Monteverde, Wood felt a sense of weight in the night, of the unknown lurking. Pearson would feel it more, if he felt anything. That didn't make Wood feel any better. Neither did Captain Vause when Wood got back to his desk.

"Not a trace," Vause said. "All he has to do is find a canyon, park, and we won't find him tonight. Maybe not for days."

"He'll have to eat, make some move."

"That's probably what we'll have to wait for," Vause said. "With that gun, I just hope he doesn't make the wrong move."

Alice was asleep in a cell. Wood lay down in the next empty cell. He was tired, but not sleepy. It was going to be a long night.

Somewhere before dawn, Wood awoke and listened to the silent city. No rain, and no birds sang. At least the floods seemed over. He went back to sleep.

In the deep dark before dawn, James Pearson walked under the trees to the rear of his big Brandwater house. He followed a trail Andrew Hoek's cattle had once used to go to water, but Pearson didn't know that. A police patrol car passed slowly out on the street. Pearson stood motionless under the trees.

The patrol car passed the dark house without stopping, and Pearson went on to the back door of his house. He went inside and stood for a time listening to the silence of the empty house. In the darkness his face was peculiarly young, as if the lines of age had faded with the years themselves. The way the insane can look young again, or those who have made some great decision.

He walked on through his formal living room with its stiff French furniture. He stopped in front of a mirror, looked at his own face in the dark room. His own youthfulness seemed to surprise him. He touched his face.

"I go tomorrow, Celia," he said. "There's a war on. I have to go, too."

He listened for an answer, looked around, and then sighed. That deep sigh of a body that needed air, oxygen-starved.

He wandered through the house, upstairs and down, like a young soldier about to go off to war. About to leave his new bride behind. On the second floor, he looked into his wife's room, aware she wasn't there, and yet somehow looking for her, too. Wanting her to be there, perhaps, to prove that nothing at all had happened after all.

"With any luck, after a while, maybe you can join me over there. If I get stationed in Japan. There's a chance, you see. I speak the language. Just a little luck."

He spoke normally, in a conversational voice, to his friends around him. To Celia. This time he didn't look around for an answer, seemed to hear voices answer, nodded.

"We can have the baby there, dear. In Japan. Yes."

He blinked at the soundless answer, turned and went downstairs again. In his small study he sat down at his desk. He studied the top of the neat desk, considering what work there was to do. He sat back in his desk chair, rubbed slowly at his face with both hands the way a man does when he hasn't been to bed all night and feels both tired and dirty.

Then he closed his eyes and sat there for some fifteen minutes. He was asleep. His handsome face lolled down toward his chest. He might have slept for hours, head down at his dark desk, but a patrol car passed again on the street, and Pearson jerked awake. His hand went into his coat pocket, came out with the Nambu pistol in it.

This time the patrol car stopped, and footsteps went around the house. Pearson jumped up, shrank into the shadows. The footsteps went all around the house, checked the locked doors, and went back to the street. The patrol car drove away.

Pearson smiled. They wouldn't find his car. He looked at the pistol in his hand. He put it down on the desk, sat down, and closed his eyes again.

He opened his eyes almost at once this time, unlocked a bottom drawer of his desk. He raised a false bottom of the drawer, took out a thin, dusty Manila folder. He read the papers in the folder one at a time, leaned forward to stare at two sheets of letter paper.

Outside, the dawn had broken, a pale gray light that outlined the eucalyptus trees and the cottage across the yard behind his study windows. Pearson sighed again, glanced at the clock on his desk. It was just before seven A.M.

He heard the footsteps. Lighter steps outside, quicker. There was the sound of a key in the front door lock. Pearson got up, went out through the dining room. He listened.

"Hello? Alan? Frieda?"

There was no answer. Pearson walked on through the dining room and into the entry hall at the front. The front door was open. Pearson frowned at the open door, rubbed his eyes, then went on into the living room and back to his study in a big circle. In the study doorway, he stopped. Something moved in a shadowy corner. Silent and watchful.

Pearson walked to his desk. He looked down at the open Manila folder.

"So you know," he said.

He sat down at the desk. He began to talk, doodling on the folder as he talked.

*

Harry Wood woke up to the sound of his name.

"Sergeant Wood?" the Duty-sergeant said. "Telephone."

Wood sat up. His watch showed almost eight o'clock. The sun was up outside the cell window. Wood shook his head.

"Who is it?"

"Old Cornelious Hook. He's pretty worked up."

Wood stood up and left the cell. Alice Garnet was out of her cell. She followed Wood to his desk in the squad room.

Wood picked up his phone. "Yes, Mr. Hook?"

"He just called me! Jim!" the old man's agitated voice said from the other end. "He sounds bad, distraught and confused. Yet cool, too. Crazy."

"Where is he?"

"He didn't say, but it was a local call. I had the impression that he was nearby. He . . . he said he had a way to settle all the trouble. He said that everything would be fine soon."

"But no hint where he could be?"

Hook was silent. "Well, I did hear a kind of echo. The kind you hear around water in large rooms. A pool, perhaps. The club pool, possibly, or Sam Garnet's house? That would be—"

"Stay where you are," Wood said, hung up.

He checked his pistol, started out of the squad room. Alice Garnet came behind him.

"I could help," she said. "I can't wait around here, Harry."

Wood nodded. "We'll try Sam's house first. He might just think it smart to hide there. Just do what I tell you."

The courthouse parking lot was filling with the morning's cars, the business of the city beginning another day. Wood and Alice hurried toward where he had parked his car. The sun was low and glaring as they pushed through the crowds of people on their way in to work.

The movement was to Wood's left behind a row of parked cars. Something flashed in the sun.

"Down!"

Wood pushed Alice sprawling to the ground.

The shots exploded. Two shots. Wood spun, was flung down as both bullets hit him.

On the ground, Alice Garnet screamed.

She scrambled up. Far to the left a car door slammed, the car squealed away to the street and was gone. Alice Garnet stared toward where the car had burnt rubber leaving.

People ran up.

Alice bent down over Harry Wood.

24

Lee Beckett, the investigator from the County Prosecutor's office, stood over Alice Garnet in the hospital corridor. Alice smoked, her copper hair disheveled and her face pale. Captain Vause came down the corridor.

"Hit twice, but lucky," Vause said. "One bullet in the left shoulder, one in the side that didn't hit anything vital. Both eight-millimeter slugs, a Nambu again."

"He say anything?"

"Mostly unprintable. He didn't see who shot."

Beckett looked down at Alice Garnet. "Did you see?"

"No," she said, shook her head. "Just someone behind the parked cars."

Vause said, "Other witnesses heard a car, didn't see it. You were closest, Miss Garnet. Did you see it?"

"No, I didn't see the car," Alice said.

Beckett studied her face. "You're sure, Miss Garnet?"

She looked for an ashtray in the corridor. "I'm sure."

"Harry was on his way to look for Pearson," Captain Vause said. "Pearson had called old Hook, said he had a way to settle all the trouble. Is he crazy enough to think everything would be okay if he killed Wood?"

"Could be," Beckett said. "Cornered, running in circles, he just might get the notion that if he stopped the hunter the hunt would end. He'd confessed to Wood, right?"

"Yes," Captain Vause said, nodded.

Beckett said to Alice Garnet, "Where was Wood going to look for Pearson?"

"Sam's house first, then the country club," Alice said.

"I wonder," Beckett said, turned to Vause. "You think it's possible that Pearson called Hook to set a trap? He knew that Hook would be sure to call Wood."

"I guess—" Vause began. He stopped when Phil Martin came along the corridor.

"We just got a call at headquarters, Captain," Martin said. "Seems there's a strange car parked out of sight near the garage of a man in Brandwater. It's a gray car, rental he thinks, and the man lives on the next block to Pearson—right behind the Pearson house."

"You go back to the squad room," Vause said.

"Okay if I work with you, Captain?" Lee Beckett said.

"I'll take any help now," Vause said.

*

In the cool, sunny Brandwater driveway, Lee Beckett examined the unknown gray car.

"Los Angeles rental car," he said. "Nothing in it."

"When did you spot it?" Vause asked the owner of the house.

"I saw it when I got up at eight-thirty," the man said. His name was Pierce, he didn't know the Pearsons well. "When it was still here at ten, I called you. I don't much like strangers using my house as a parking lot."

"The engine's cold," Beckett said.

They told Pierce to stay in his house, made their way

carefully across the back yards to the big Pearson house. It was silent in the January morning, no cars near it. Both policemen had their guns out. Beckett checked the garage. Only the red Jaguar was inside. Beckett went in and checked the hood of the Jaguar. It was still warm.

"Been driven within the last few hours," Beckett said.

They approached the front door warily. It was unlocked. Inside the house nothing moved. The entrance hall was cold out of the winter sun. All the shades were drawn in the dim and silent mansion. Vause went through the living room and that side of the house. Beckett did the dining room side. They met in the small, book-lined study.

Beckett saw him first.

"Captain!"

Two shoes, trousers and a bare ankle protruded from behind the desk in the study. The desk chair had fallen over.

Both men looked down behind the desk.

James Pearson lay on his back, the desk chair near him. A pool of blood was almost dry. A Nambu automatic pistol was on the floor inches from the dead man's right hand.

Beckett kneeled down over the dead Pearson. Captain Vause picked up the Nambu carefully by the barrel with a handkerchief.

"One shot in the heart, it looks like," Beckett said. "Jaw and neck are rigid, arms a little. Maybe two to four hours. Say from maybe seven A.M. to maybe nine A.M."

"Gun's got three bullets missing," Vause said. "Two in Harry Wood, one in himself."

"Yeh," Beckett said.

Captain Vause went to call his men and the Coroner. Lee Beckett walked around the small study. The desk was neat, but one drawer was open at the bottom, and a Manila folder lay open on the desk. A copy of Sarah Pearson's birth certificate was in the folder, various medical reports on her as an infant, the agreement made in 1952 for the L.A. sanitarium to take care of her, and many bills.

The bare surface of the folder was covered with doodling. A single word over and over: *Sarah, Sarah, Sarah, Sarah* . . . Some of the names had been outlined, filled in, the way a man will do while he is thinking or talking, abstracted.

Beckett turned back to the body, looked all around it. Captain Vause returned, watched Beckett searching.

"No note," Beckett said. "Just the name: Sarah."

"Maybe that's the note."

A big car turned into the driveway and stopped. Too soon for the Coroner or Vause's men. The front door opened and closed.

"Jim!"

The call echoed through the big house. Cornelius Hook's voice. The old man's heavy step came toward the study. Beckett went to the study door.

"I know you," Cornelius Hook said. "Beckett, right? From Tucker's office. So, is my son-in-law here?"

"Mr. Hook—" Beckett began.

The old man brushed Beckett aside, went on into the study. He walked to the desk, looked down at James Pearson.

"So he did it," Hook said.

*

Cornelius Hook said, "I suppose it's for the best."

It was next afternoon. They had taken the bullets out of Wood, bandaged his side and shoulder, strapped his left arm to his chest, and he had slept eighteen hours. Now he sat up in the hospital bed and listened to Lee Beckett. Captain Vause and old Hook were in the room, too.

"The way it was, I guess so," Vause agreed.

Wood said, "Any suicide note?"

"No," Beckett said. "Just this folder open on his desk. A lot of old documents about Sarah Pearson. He doodled her name all over the folder. I guess she was on his mind."

Wood took the folder with his good hand. He studied it.

"I wonder if he was alone in the house all the time?" Wood said. "You doodle like that when you talk, or listen."

"Or when you brood, Sergeant," Cornelius Hook said.

Wood lay back on his pillows. "What's the Coroner and the lab say, Captain?"

"Single gunshot wound in the heart," Vause said. "Between seven and nine A.M. that morning. Gun was the Nambu we found, same gun used on you and Roberta Dunn."

"He hid his rental car, called Mr. Hook about seven-thirty or forty," Wood said. "He got his Jaguar, drove downtown, shot me about eight, drove back to his house, and shot himself?"

Beckett said, "He must have called Hook from near headquarters. A trap to make you come out. Alice Garnet saw the red Jaguar. She lied at first, but admits now she saw the Jag. She knows the car."

"Yeh," Wood said. He was silent for a moment. "A trap. But no note to tell why it all happened. The original motive. What Yukio Ikeda knew for his blackmail twelve years ago."

"He murdered to hide it," Vause said. "Why tell now?"

"I suppose you're right, Captain," Wood said.

Cornelius Hook said, "I've tried to think. Perhaps some possible scandal in Japan, or later. My daughter owns the stock in the company, I made sure of that. A man has needs, makes mistakes, but I wouldn't have stood for a scandal that hurt Celia."

"Why did you go to Pearson's house, Mr. Hook?" Wood asked. "You were supposed to wait with Alan and Jitsuko."

"After Jim called, Alan decided to drive down to the sanitarium to see Celia—and to see if Jim might have gone down there. When I heard what had happened to you, I called Vause. They told me he was at Jim's house. I was uneasy."

"How are the Thesigers?"

"George is resting at home," Hook said.

"His vice-presidency waiting," Wood said. "Are Alan and Jitsuko back?"

"I expect I'd better see," Hook said. At the door, he looked back. "Someone will have to tell Celia." The tone of his voice said he didn't want it to be him, but he guessed it would be. A strong old man. "Get well, Sergeant, then come and talk to me. George Thesiger can't run our security department."

The door closed behind Hook, and Wood turned his eyes to Captain Vause and Beckett.

"In the heart is a hard way to shoot yourself," Wood said. "Why shoot me if he planned to kill himself?"

Beckett said, "Maybe you were too close to that initial motive. He still wanted to hide it, protect someone."

After Beckett and Captain Vause had gone, Wood lit his first cigarette since he'd been shot. He was still smoking it when Alice Garnet came in. She sat some distance from the bed.

"I'm sorry," she said.

Wood smoked. She took her own cigarette from her handbag.

"I saw the Jaguar, and I lied. I knew the car. He could have killed you, and I protected him."

"You saw the Jaguar," Wood said.

"I tried to bribe you. Not for Hook. Money and me to turn away, leave Donny alone. Let him go."

"Love doesn't end in a minute. You protected him, it's natural." Wood looked toward her. "What I wonder about is who Pearson was still protecting? You're sure you don't know what it was Yukio Ikeda came to blackmail about?"

"No," she said. "I don't."

Wood stared at the far wall beyond the foot of his bed. A blank white wall in the afternoon sunlight.

"Blood money," he said.

"What?"

"Twelve years ago Yukio Ikeda got drunk, said something odd to Vinnie Tugela—'Bloodwater pays blood money.' Ikeda laughed."

"What does it mean, Harry?"

"Pearson was doodling Sarah's name before he shot himself. I'm not sure he was alone the whole time in his house."

She put out her cigarette, came to the bed. "Harry, does it really matter this time? He confessed, he's dead. He shot you."

"Me, too," Wood said. "If Pearson hadn't confessed and run, I could have taken that bribe." He lay back on the pillows. "Thesiger won't make waves, a cozy job. Hook thinks it's all for the best. Vause, Sheriff Hoag and Tucker are relieved, Pearson saved a mess. Beckett's a practical man. I think I could be Hook's security chief. Let it ride, use what I can't change."

"Can you change much, Harry?"

"You never know. I might even help change what happened to Sarah Pearson. She's the real victim—of all the safe, smug and comfortable who let it all slide."

Alice bent down, kissed him. He held her with his good arm. Then he let her go, and she left. In the silent hospital room, Wood smoked another cigarette. Then he picked up the telephone, put in a call to Lieutenant Shimada down in Los Angeles.

*

Two hours later, just before dark, Wood dressed and slipped out of the hospital. At headquarters, he waved off the protests at his leaving the hospital too soon, talked to Phil Martin and Diaz in the lab. He inspected the contents of James Pearson's pockets.

He drove to the big Pearson house. The housekeeper, Frieda, was back, but no one else. Wood talked to her, then searched the small library and Pearson's bedroom. Out in the garage he checked over the red Jaguar.

Then he got into his car and drove south on the freeway toward Los Angeles. He drove slowly in the right lane. He had only one good arm to work with.

25

In the sanitarium office the doctor shook his head sadly.
"We heard about Mr. Pearson. A terrible thing."
"His murders, too?" Wood said.
The doctor looked uncomfortable, but his mouth set firmly. His job didn't include judging people. Wood sat facing him.
"I want to see Mrs. Pearson," he said.
"Absolutely not!"
"You can't do it, Doctor. Don't risk it now. Alan Pearson is still around, isn't he? Okay, get him here. He's family."
The doctor reached for his telephone, spoke briefly. Then he sat silent. They waited. This time someone laughed crazily somewhere off in the white corridors. The doctor didn't seem to hear, he'd worked with the sick and lost too long. Five minutes later Alan Pearson came in. Jitsuko Ikeda was still with him.
"Staying close to your mother?" Wood said.
"We're in a motel across the road, yes," Alan said.
"I want to see her," Wood said.
"No," Alan said.

"Before your father shot himself he wasn't alone. In that study he was talking to someone. About your sister. Talking, and thinking, and doodling Sarah's name over and over."

The doctor said, "It won't help you, Sergeant. Celia Pearson is totally psychotic now. Catatonic. She can't even speak."

Wood nodded. "Why did that happen, Doctor?"

"I really can't—" the doctor began.

"Sure you can," Wood said. "When did she—?"

Alan Pearson said, "Let him see her. Let him!"

"Now," Wood said.

The doctor got up, led them down the corridors. To still a third wing of the sanitarium this time. Neither where Celia Pearson had been, nor where Sarah Pearson lay in her dark and vegetable world. A locked wing, and a locked room. The doctor unlocked the room door.

In this room there was no furniture. The windows were barred, the floor and walls heavily padded.

"We're going to transfer her. We can't handle her now."

Celia Pearson sat on the padded floor in a corner, her knees up, her head down. Her black dress looked like it hadn't been changed in days. Dark stains on it, some small rips.

"Mrs. Pearson?" Wood said.

"She doesn't even know we're here," the doctor said.

Alan said, "Satisfied, Sergeant?"

The boy's voice was strangled and bitter—his father was dead, his mother insane, and his never-known sister a deformed horror. Wood didn't look at him. Instead, he crossed the padded floor to Celia Pearson. He bent and began to search her.

"What the hell—!" Alan began.

The doctor said, "She can't feel him, Alan."

Wood said nothing, went on touching the silent woman who sat rigid in her corner. The faint rustle of paper was loud in the padded room. Wood spoke without turning:

"You haven't undressed her since she got back?"

"She fought us," the doctor said. "Best left alone."

Wood reached inside the frozen woman's dress. She jerked back, and her fists began to pound on the padded wall. Wood stood up. He held two crumpled sheets of paper.

"I talked to Lieutenant Shimada of the Osaka police," Wood said. "He talked to Tanaka Instruments over there. Did you know about it, Alan?"

"No," Alan said. "I never knew. None of it."

Celia Pearson was motionless again. Rigid in her corner, her head down as if it would never come up. They all left.

*

The doctor sat in his chair behind his desk. Wood sat across from him. Jitsuko sat in a corner. Alan Pearson stood, paced.

"The doctor called my grandfather about midnight that night," Alan said. "Two nights ago, after my father escaped from you."

"Mrs. Pearson had been much better," the doctor said. "We let her watch television in the recreation room. We were all busy with the flooding. She must have just walked out. Someone drove her to the bus depot. When we found her gone, we checked. She'd taken the Monteverde bus. I called Mr. Pearson at once, got no answer. So I called Mr. Hook."

Alan paced. "Grandfather found Mother just sitting in

the bus depot, brought her home. Suko and I were asleep. We knew nothing about it until Grandfather's houseman woke me up. He told me Grandfather wanted me at my house right away. I got Suko—"

"What time was this?" Wood asked.

"About eight-ten, we got to my house about eight-fifteen," Alan said. "My father . . . my father was dead, shot. My mother had shot him! Grandfather had found her. She'd left Grandfather's house, gone home, found Dad, and shot him! Grandfather had discovered her gone, guessed where she'd go, followed her. Too late. She'd—" The boy shook his head.

"Yeh," Wood said. "Your father wasn't planning suicide, he was dreaming of escape. No note. The heart is an awkward place to shoot yourself. Try it sometime. Why would a man who intended suicide try to kill me first? It didn't make sense. Only why did your grandfather tell you? He could have lied to you the way he's lied to everyone else to protect Mrs. Pearson."

"He needed our help, wanted us to help protect her."

"Yeh," Wood said again. "Where was she when you arrived?"

"Upstairs asleep. Grandfather had given her Seconal."

"Had your father been dead long?"

"I don't know," Alan said. "A while, I guess. Mother was so deep asleep she didn't wake up all the way back down here."

Jitsuko said, very low, "I have seen dead people. In Japan. Mr. Pearson had been dead perhaps an hour. There was no way Mr. Hook or Alan could have saved him."

"So you drove your mother down here?" Wood said.

Alan nodded. "In Grandfather's other car, my Porsche is

too small. Grandfather said Mother had suffered enough, we couldn't help Dad. He said we'd drive her back here, say nothing, and he'd make Dad's death look like suicide. He did, and drove home in my Porsche. The doctor didn't know, and we thought that with Dad a suicide, no one would ever ask. But—" The boy's haunted eyes looked up. "Does it have to come out, Sergeant? I mean, what will it help?"

"I'm not sure," Wood said. He held the two crumpled papers in his hand. "I'm surprised Hook didn't destroy these."

"We didn't know Mother had them," Alan said. "I guess Dad was looking at them, Mother came in and read them, and—"

"The Tanaka valve," Wood said. "Your father built his success, his life, on it. Built it all on Sarah."

Wood looked at the two papers. "An American officer, more powerful than a bunch of poor Japanese fishermen. So the chemical company in Uta-Kaze made a deal, and your father took it. The choice he talked about. Hurt no one. After all, Sarah couldn't be helped, could she? Stupid to turn down a wonderful opportunity. So your father listened to Hook, made his deal."

The doctor toyed with a pencil. Alan Pearson seemed to be seeing his father back then, seeing the tragedy of his sister, thinking, perhaps, of what he, Alan, would have done. Jitsuko seemed to be seeing something even farther away.

"Two letters," Wood said, looking at the papers he had taken from Celia Pearson's dress. "Tanaka is tied to the chemical company in Uta-Kaze, so they offered the exclusive American license for their valve if your father would sign a full release for Sarah's damages. A million-dollar chance, good business. So the second letter settles all legal claims for a token compensation of a thousand dollars."

Wood laid the letters aside. "The chemical company is safe, your father and grandfather have the valve. Blood money from bloodwater. Bought on Sarah's horror. But your mother had already broken down over Sarah. What would she do if she knew about the deal? Then Yukio Ikeda found copies of the two letters at Tanaka Instrument, and he learned of Celia's breakdowns. So he came to blackmail—your father pays him, or he shows the two letters to your mother."

Jitsuko was crying. "Terrible, my brother! And me? I—"

"No," Alan said. "He was just weak. You, too, Suko. You both listened to people like my grandfather. We all do. We listen to the practical men. Sarah was poisoned by that water, but so were all of us. Yukio, Garnet, my father and mother, Miss Dunn, and you and me. Bloodwater."

The girl cried silently. Alan didn't go to her, touch her, but somehow his voice did. It changed, low and soft.

"You came to blackmail," Alan said. "Okay, I guessed that pretty early. But I love you. I think you changed because you came to love me. My grandfather would say no, never risk being cheated, never trust, never be a sucker. But someone has to say yes, risk being a fool and a sucker, or we'll never break the chains. I don't want to be poisoned. I want to love you, try to live. Suko, do you love me? Will you try?"

She was suddenly nervous. "I love you, but—"

"Okay, then we'll try. We'll go to Mexico and find out, give it a chance. I won't lose you because I won't risk being a fool. We won't listen to my grandfather anymore."

The girl nodded, nothing more.

"Poor Dad," Alan said. "To live with something so terrible he had to murder to hide it."

Wood said, "Sam Garnet, your grandfather, those chemical executives in Japan, and a lot of other people wouldn't have thought the deal bad enough for blackmail or murder. But your father did. For himself, and for your mother. Sure she'd go crazy if she ever knew they were living on Sarah's horror."

Wood stood up. "He was right, too. She did go crazy. And she killed him."

26

Harry Wood reached Brandwater before midnight. The rich suburb built on old Andrew Hoek's long-ago farm was dark and proper now that the creeks were down and the flood danger over. No more blood from the water here. Cornelius Hook's house wasn't dark, a light in the glass-walled study. Alan and Jitsuko had called the old man before they drove down to Mexico to see if there could be a chance for them.

Old Hook sat in his high-backed chair. "They went to Mexico?"

"They could make it together," Wood said. "She loves him."

He stood across the warm study from Hook. The houseman had brought him a whisky. Wood drank it.

"Do you have to reveal that Celia killed Jim?" Hook said. "I'd like to talk about our security chief position."

"Me and Sam Garnet. You buy everyone, Mr. Hook?"

"When I must," Hook said. "To correct mistakes, keep control. Jim was a murderer three times over, almost four."

"Cheaper to buy people than change your methods? The way it's cheaper for that chemical company in Uta-Kaze to pay off the maimed than to clean up their mercury waste?"

"My daughter is important. She may still recover."

Wood drank. "Maybe it doesn't have to all come out."

Hook leaned forward like a hunter in the saddle who sees his quarry close ahead. "You could go far at Hook Instrument. Jim Pearson caused it all. Panicked twelve years ago."

"So you did know about Yukio Ikeda all along."

"Only after it was over back then. I'd have handled it better if I'd known in advance. Twelve years ago Jim lost his head, this time he went soft. If he'd let Garnet get rid of the Ikeda girl before anyone knew who she was, none of this would have happened. Celia would still be sane, three people would be alive, the family safe! I can't protect from every weakness."

"Two people would still be alive," Wood said.

"Have you forgotten Roberta Dunn?"

"No, I haven't forgotten Miss Dunn. I haven't forgotten myself, either," Wood said. "Jim Pearson didn't kill Miss Dunn, and he didn't shoot me."

Cornelius Hook sat back slowly. "No? Then who did, Sergeant?"

"You did, Mr. Hook."

The old man found a cigar in his pocket.

"Can you prove that?"

"You know," Wood said, "I don't know if I can or not."

Hook lit the cigar, drew on it until it glowed.

"The time doesn't work if Pearson shot me," Wood said. "I was shot about eight A.M. downtown. At eight-fifteen, Alan says Pearson had been dead nearly an hour; so does Jitsuko. Mrs. Pearson was asleep at eight-fifteen. Even Seconal takes time to work, especially on someone as wrought up as she must have been. You say Pearson shot me at eight, got back to his house and was shot by Celia. You found them, called Alan, and Celia was asleep when he got there. All in fifteen minutes? I don't think so."

"What do you think?" Hook said, studied his cigar.

"Celia shot Pearson about seven-fifteen. You arrived just after, saw Pearson was dead. You drugged Celia, drove downtown, called me from a pay phone, shot me when I came out. Then you drove back to Pearson's house, called Alan, faked the suicide.

"Pearson had no reason to shoot me. But you had Celia to protect after she shot Pearson. I might arrive at the house at any moment. Shooting me would delay the police long enough for you to get Celia away and phony the suicide. Shooting me would keep the real motive hidden, maybe, and protect Celia more. If I died, you might manage to hide it all. Pearson and suicide, case closed, real motive never known."

"I should have been a better shot," Hook said.

"Then there's Roberta Dunn. Pearson had killed Sam Garnet to stop any more murders. He wouldn't have shot Miss Dunn. But you knew what happened to Yukio Ikeda, you knew Alan thought Miss Dunn might have seen something back then, so you shot her."

"Did I?"

"That Nambu killed her and Pearson, and shot me. Celia got the Nambu from Pearson to shoot him, and you got it from her to shoot me. But it's your gun. I saw Pearson find it behind the books in your library—*after* Roberta Dunn had been killed."

Hook blew smoke. "Jim knew where it was. He probably took it earlier, then put it back."

"Possible," Wood said, "but there's the Jaguar, too. Why

Wood said, "You couldn't leave it alone, the way you couldn't leave Jim Pearson alone twenty-two years ago. That started it, Mr. Hook. Not Pearson—you. You began it all by convincing Pearson that Sarah's horror was an opportunity he could use for his own advantage. You could have stopped it all anywhere along the way these last days. Instead, you thought only about the advantage of your family, made it worse, and changed nothing."

Hook smiled. "You don't like me, Sergeant. But I don't really care what you think."

"I know you don't," Wood said.

*

When Alice Garnet opened her apartment door the next morning, Harry Wood strode in past her. The late January sun was bright through the windows. Wood told her about Hook.

"You found the Jaguar keys?"

"Blood on his jacket that morning, he changed it as soon as he got home. The keys were in the pocket."

"So he'll go to prison? The whole family destroyed?"

"Who knows? He's got money and the best lawyers. He'll fight. No guilty conscience for Hook. He's not Jim Pearson."

"Conscience? Is that what happened?"

"Pearson grabbed an opportunity back then, believed it was right, Sarah couldn't be helped," Wood said. "But inside he was torn up. All the years part of him was sure he'd done only what he should have, and part of him condemned himself for living on Sarah's tragedy and Celia's suffering. When Sam was going to kill Jitsuko, he broke inside. Guilt, shame, horror. He loved his first child, felt he'd betrayed her, denied her pain. Those last doodles tell it—

would Pearson change cars to one known to be his own? It was no gain for him, even if he was thinking that straight. No, he'd have used the rental car, but you didn't know where it was. You had only your own car or the Jag. Besides, you figured that if the Jag was seen, Pearson would look even more guilty of being the one who'd shot me."

"Thin, Sergeant, all of it. Mostly supposition."

"Maybe enough," Wood said. "With your motive, and Alan's testimony about the time. Your houseman probably knows you left this house earlier than you say. With you in jail he'll talk, I think. Alice Garnet will tell her story of the bribe offer to me. We'll try to use George Thesiger's beating, show your violence. Thesiger may deny it, but Vinnie Tugela will make a deal and talk.

"Of course, you'll say Alice Garnet was bribing me on her own to save Pearson, her lover, and Tugela's not a good witness on character. Your lawyers will work him over, work on Alan and Jitsuko, too."

"I have very good lawyers," Hook said.

"Still, juries can be funny. You never do know what they'll see and accept, what will convince them."

"Are you arresting me then, Sergeant?"

Wood nodded. "I'm taking you in now. You made one more mistake. I went all over the Jaguar, all over Pearson's study and bedroom, checked all that was found on his body. I can't find the keys to the Jaguar. I guess you dropped them into your pocket by reflex when you got back in the Jaguar from shooting me. A common habit, automatic. We'll find them in one of your jacket pockets after you're in jail."

"Well, then I suppose I'll see you in court," Hook said. He stood up, slowly and heavily.

Sarah, Sarah, Sarah. Only I don't think he ever really knew what had gone wrong for him."

Alice watched the dust in the streams of sun. "So it's over."

"Not quite," Wood said.

Alice looked at him. She got up and went into the kitchen. She poured two cups of coffee. From the couch, Wood watched her.

"Alan and Jitsuko have gone to Mexico," Wood said. "To see if they can make it together. He's an honest kid, strong. He said someone has to say yes and try to live. Take a chance."

She brought Wood his coffee, sat down near him.

"You said you'd marry me," he said. "Will you?"

"You still want me?"

"You loved a man for twenty years. What else would you do but try to help him? Call it habit, memory, even love. If you hadn't tried, you wouldn't be human. I'd want the same for me."

"Would you, Harry?"

"Yes, I would," he said. "If I could have trusted Hook, or things had worked out differently, I might have taken a bribe."

"No, you wouldn't have."

"You're so sure?"

"Yes."

"I'm not," Wood said. He drank his coffee. "Only, if I'd taken it, we'd gone away, what would I have done all day?"

"A cop's wife," she said. "Are *you* sure, Harry?"

"You remember when you told Pearson you didn't want to go with him? That was before you knew he'd killed anyone. You meant it. That's enough for us to try."

"Then I'll marry you," Alice said. "Yes."

They sat there for a time, smiling. Then Wood got up. With his one good hand, he touched her. Only the touch.

"They owe me a week or so off," he said.

"I'll be here," Alice Garnet said.